EXILE FROM JAMESTOWN

EXILE FROM JAMESTOWN

Arnie P. Zimbelman

iUniverse, Inc.
New York Lincoln Shanghai

EXILE from JAMESTOWN

Copyright © 2005 by Arnie P. Zimbelman

All rights reserved. No part of this book may be used or reproduced by any means, graphic, electronic, or mechanical, including photocopying, recording, taping or by any information storage retrieval system without the written permission of the publisher except in the case of brief quotations embodied in critical articles and reviews.

iUniverse books may be ordered through booksellers or by contacting:

iUniverse
2021 Pine Lake Road, Suite 100
Lincoln, NE 68512
www.iuniverse.com
1-800-Authors (1-800-288-4677)

Cover Graphic: Courtesy Colonial Williamsburg Foundation

ISBN-13: 978-0-595-34898-5 (pbk)
ISBN-13: 978-0-595-79615-1 (ebk)
ISBN-10: 0-595-34898-X (pbk)
ISBN-10: 0-595-79615-X (ebk)

Printed in the United States of America

Dedication:

Once more, to Iris

* * * * * * *

And those who came were resolved to be Englishmen,
Gone to the world's end, but English every one,
And they ate the white corn-kernels, parched in the sun,
And they knew it not, but they'd not be English again.

—Stephen Vincent Benet

* * * * * * *

Acknowledgements

Special thanks go to my daughters, Deborah Hirsch, Terrie St.Clair, and Sherrie Zimbelman, for their interest and encouragement as this work progressed. Terrie, a former editor, was particularly helpful, spending endless hours in meticulous review and checking of punctuation, etc. Our son-in-law, Dr. Theodore Omtzigt, provided the electronic wizardry necessary to forward the manuscript for publication. Most of all, however, I owe a limitless debt of gratitude to my wife Iris who patiently deciphered my hand-written scribblings, typed them into workable text, and served as my perceptive editor, gentle critic, and constant cheerleader.

Chapter 1

A soft early morning breeze gently billowed the white canvas sails of the three small wooden ships as they proceeded on their north-by-northwesterly course, seeking the elusive coastline. The light of early dawn gradually brightened, bringing a rising rumble of anticipation from anxious sailors who completely lined the ships' railings or swung from the rigging above. Now that they realized how *near* they were to the end of their perilous journey, every eye focused westward as each man strove to be *first* to detect their ultimate destination. After all, Captain Newport had promised a rich reward to the one who would initially sight that coveted goal: he was to be awarded the very first *nugget of gold* found in the new land!

From his vantage point high in the rigging of the "Susan Constant," Geoffry Payne strained like the others to catch that primary glimpse of the land which was their long-sought destination. *Virginia!* The very name was alluring, mystical, carrying with it fond memories of their dear departed sovereign, the beloved Queen Elizabeth. Geoffry smiled, recalling how Elizabeth had been referred to affectionately as "Good Queen Bess," or the "Virgin Queen," and that the enchanted land they were now seeking, the land that offered so much hope and such grand promise, had been named in her honor.

"D'ya see anythin' yet, mate?" Geoffry heard someone call out.

"Nah, it's still too dark. But it can't be much farther now, that's for sure."

"Hah! I been hearin' that fer days, I has. I'm beginnin' to wonder if there really *is* such a place as this here Virginia!"

"Oh, it's there, alright. Just keep a sharp lookout, and keep thinking about all that gold! And don't forget, I aim to spot Virginia before *anyone else* does!"

Perhaps almost as alluring as the expected monetary reward, in Geoffry's mind, was the sense of anticipation that, at long last, they were nearing the end of their tedious, weary weeks aboard the cramped little sailing vessels. Each man, he knew, was filled with expectancy and excitement at the prospect that soon their tiny fleet would successfully reach the promised "golden land." Then it would be only a brief matter of days before all aboard would surely achieve their own personal goal: instant wealth, wealth far greater than even their most fanciful imaginations could comprehend! As the men had come to believe from tales repeated endlessly during the difficult days of passage, the moment their ships reached Virginia, they had only to load them with cargoes of plentiful gold, just as the Spanish had been doing for years. Then they would all return home to a life of everlasting luxury! Still, the desire to be *first* to view this magical, life-altering paradise was compelling!

Geoffry Payne knew that he too harbored many of the same ambitions that motivated the rest of the crewmembers. Still, as his eyes continued their watchful sweep of the distant horizon, his mind gradually drifted back over the momentous series of events that had brought him finally to this particular place, at this particular time. Could it really be *true*, he wondered? Was it *possible* that he was now an actual part of an adventure so daring, so bold in scope, so magnificent as to overshadow all that had gone before in the entire realm of his consciousness?

Born in the Wiltshire County village of Salisbury in southern England, Geoffry was the second son of a skilled stone mason. His father's duties involved constant evaluation and repair of the town's landmark cathedral, noted for its lofty and elegant 404-foot spire. Early on, Geoffry had seemed destined to follow his father's trade, as his older brother Derik had done. In fact, the younger son had actually become a rather accomplished stone worker himself. But even as Geoffry's skills increased, they were accompanied by a dawning realization: this was not what he envisioned as his life's work! His restless, adventuresome spirit craved *more* than the comfort and security offered by the charming village of his birth. He had gradually come to realize that he expected more, much more, from life.

And so, despite his family's dire warnings and misgivings, Geoffry had left Salisbury for the coastal town of Portsmouth. Here, working at odd jobs around the bustling docks frequented by trading ships from exotic ports ~ ports whose names were totally unfamiliar and thus totally irresistible to the eager young dock-worker ~ he had come to a new awareness of just how limited and limiting his previous existence had been. The world outside the safe confines of his native Salisbury offered excitement, opportunity! And if reaching out to attain it required acceptance of an increased element of risk and danger, it only served to make the whole even more enticing.

Twenty-four years old, tall for the times at nearly six feet in height, trim and fit with muscles hardened by years of lifting and shaping heavy stone, possessed of a seemingly limitless good nature, Geoffry had quickly become a favorite along the docks. His dark, flashing eyes, along with a temperament that frequently brought a hasty response to any perceived injustice, any insult or threat whether real or imagined, were traits said to be inherited from his Irish mother. His "Irish temper" was known to flare easily. It was balanced, however, by an equally ready smile and by a genuinely open, accepting attitude toward almost everyone. Ships' captains sought him out when it came time to load or unload their cargoes since he had proved to be a steady, dependable worker.

Gradually he had enhanced his nautical skills and knowledge. He assisted with ships' rigging, helped to repair sails, scraped barnacles clinging tenaciously to wooden hulls, and performed a host of other essential tasks, all without hesitation or complaint. Twice he had been permitted to sail along as part of the crew on short journeys to nearby ports. From these experiences, an emerging desire to explore vistas ever farther afield had first been kindled. He longed for far distant destinations, places still unknown and unspoiled.

It was on the second of these brief local voyages, Geoffry recalled, that he had caught that initial inkling ~ more of a rumor, actually ~ of an enterprise which was to alter totally the entire course of his future. As his trading ship had made its late night return to Portsmouth, Geoffry was standing at the rail, admiring the starry expanse of a seemingly limitless sky above, watching with never-ending fascination the play of bright phosphorescence sparkling past the ship's prow as it cut through the dark Channel waters. A fellow crewman joined him, and also observed silently for a time. He then informed Geoffry in a hushed, almost conspiratorial tone: "Well, mate, looks like this here'll be my last trip on this ol' tub, it does."

Surprised, Geoffry had inquired, "Oh? How's that? I always figured old Cap'n Teeter to be a good sailing master, honest and fair. Why take a chance on someone new?"

The sailor had moved closer. "Oh, I got no gripe with the Cap'n, I ain't. He's been right good to me, he has, an' that's a fact. It's just that I been hearin' things…," his voice trailed off.

"What kind of things? The Captain's not in some sort of trouble, is he?"

"No, no, nothin' like that. It's just that…," he looked around to make sure they were alone. "Can ya keep a secret, mate?"

"Yeah, I guess, as well as any man."

"Well, I been hearin' 'bout a new tradin' company what's settin' up over in London, I has. It's called the London Company, naturally, and I heard they needs sailors for some special kinda voyage. And the pay's to be somethin' fierce, it is."

"Where's this 'special voyage' going to go?"

The sailor had looked around again, then leaned even closer. "I heard it's goin' over to the New World, it is! You know, over to a place called Virginia. It ain't far from where them Spanish devils been findin' all o' *their* gold, it ain't! *Ship loads* o' gold, and no end in sight!" He had paused for a moment, as if to emphasize the importance of his next point. "Now I reckon this here London Company figures it's high time for us good Englishmen to step in and get *our* share o' the wealth, it is. And when they do, I means to find a way to sail right along with 'em, sure enough, or my name ain't Billy Bascomb!"

Geoffry remembered vividly the surge of excitement he had felt as he heard those words. It all made sense! After all, he knew that English "sea-dogs" like Sir John Hawkins and Francis Drake had been harassing the Spanish for years, pillaging their galleons loaded with the wealth of the New World as those ships returned to Spain. He knew, too, that "Good Queen Bess" had consistently refused to halt this piratical brigandage. In fact, rumor had it that she sometimes secretly helped to *finance* these "sea-dogs," then *shared* in a portion of the "spoils!" It had been at least partially for this reason that the Spanish had finally sent out their supposedly "Invincible Armada" in 1588 to invade England. They would punish these thieving perpetrators, and at the same time return the island once more to the true Catholic faith.

Even now, as he thought of those dark, fearful days, Geoffry could recall the almost universal wave of alarm, the near panic that had engulfed England when word spread that the Spanish Armada was actually on its way. He had been a mere lad, not yet six years of age at the time. But the fear engendered in the general English citizenry as they learned of the impending disaster had left a mark not soon forgotten. Rumor fed upon rumor regarding the size and strength of this "irresistible" invasion fleet mustered by the Spanish. Day after day throughout that anxious spring and summer, every newspaper, every posted notice had screamed of the dangers facing their "right little isle."

Then, when the Spanish Armada had finally made its belated appearance in July of 1588, all of the exaggerated fears seemed to pale in comparison to the *reality* of the military might displayed by their determined foe. It was awesome, truly overwhelming! Early reports had indicated that the Armada might number as many as eighty ships of war. That estimate had soon increased to one hundred. But ultimately, the actual true tally proved to be one hundred and thirty Spanish vessels, carrying an invasion force of 30,000 soldiers. Huge red crosses emblazoned on the sails of the massive ships had been designed to send an additional message: this was also to be a "crusade" to return Protestant England to the true faith she had abandoned under King Henry VIII. Once again, terror had swept through the populace, both in the cities and in the countryside.

It was at this critical juncture that the intrepid English naval forces had at last come into their own. Against all odds, their small, resolute fleet, manned by plucky and resourceful seamen, had totally routed their truly formidable foe. Aided further by advantageous storms, the final defeat had been sweeping, thorough, and complete!

Geoffry experienced once again the wave of intense pride, the flood of patriotic fervor that had swept over every Englishman at word of this unlikely victory. Every town and hamlet was filled with boisterous rejoicing. Parades and celebrations abounded. He couldn't suppress a chuckle as he thought of the special commemorative coin his father had later purchased, inscribed *"Venit, Vidit, Fugit"* ~ "It came, it saw, it fled." But he realized also that it had been this destruction of Spanish sea power, right there in the very Channel where he had later sailed so calmly and serenely on an English trading ship, that had opened the door for possible English expansion into the New World.

Now, as he swung from the rigging above other equally anxious sailors, with many more straining eagerly at the rail, he remembered also the elation he had felt when he had finally made his own life-altering decision: yes, he *would* join Billy Bascomb! He too would make his way to London to become part of the London Company's great venture!

Accompanied by his new acquaintance, Geoffry had managed to work his way to the beckoning metropolis. After weeks filled with disheartening false starts and disappointments, the pair had at last managed to achieve their objective. Both had been "signed on" as members of the select group of one hundred and twenty adventurous souls who would travel to the "New World," willing to risk all for a chance at glory and honor ~ as well as for the potential of unlimited personal wealth.

They had learned that there were to be three small ships in their "fleet." The "Susan Constant" would be the largest, though not particularly impressive at a mere one hundred tons. Even smaller were the "Godspeed" and the pinnace "Discovery," each a paltry forty tons. Geoffry and Billy had not yet met on a personal level the man who would lead this entire expedition of discovery, Captain

Christopher Newport, but they had seen him repeatedly bustling about the docks, shouting directions and overseeing every detail of the preparations.

The Captain's reputation for naval expertise was widely known, and was based on a solid and distinguished naval career. But Billy Bascomb had also made a point of letting Geoffry know that there was *another* side to the Captain's character.

"See that fine gentleman over there, in the handsome uniform?" Billy had asked when they first saw the Captain pacing the docks. Both took a brief break from their seemingly endless task of loading supplies into the hold of the "Susan Constant" to observe the officer. "That there's Cap'n Newport, it is. He's in charge o' *ever'thin'!* And a right good man for the job, too, I tell ya. Sure knows how to tickle the fancy o' them Spanish dogs, he does, and no mistake!"

"Oh? What do you mean, Billy?"

"Ya mean you ain't heard how he captured that there Spanish treasure ship called the 'Mader Dee,' or somethin' like that? Richest prize what was ever took by one o' our trusty lads, it was."

"You mean the 'Madre de Dios', the 'Mother of God'? Are you saying *Captain Newport's* the one who took her, Billy? Yeah, I remember hearing all about that when it happened. Word spread all the way to Salisbury. That was something, all right! I understand the Queen herself got a goodly share of the loot, too."

"Serves them greedy Spaniards right, it does," Billy concluded. "Now it's high time for us good Englishmen to get *some more* o' their gold for ourselves, it is!" He had chuckled gleefully at the thought as he and Geoffry returned to their labors.

Chapter 2

▼

Smiling quietly at his memories of this rather convoluted chain of events, Geoffry nonetheless maintained a sharp watch for the shoreline that was the object of their quest. After all, it would represent a successful "first step" in their undertaking. And he knew that the prestige resulting from being *first* to discover that momentous goal would be almost equal to the pride in being awarded the first nugget of gold. Their journey in search of this strange new land had been long and arduous, but now *nothing* seemed to matter more than to be alert, to catch that initial glimpse of their destination.

An abrupt rough jostling amongst the anxious sailors lining the rail, accompanied by the intrusion of a loud, rasping voice issuing belligerent threats, broke the mood of rapt attention.

"Git over, I says! Gimme room here, will ya, ya mangy scum, a'fore I cracks yer heads! Wanna git yerselves throwed overboard, does ya? Make way there, make room fer ol' Pike, ya hear, or ya'll certain wisht ya had!"

It was Clem Perliss, known to all aboard as "Pike," brusquely forcing his way through the line of assembled sailors.

"Hey, that was *my* place."

"Who do ya think you are, anyway, you big blockhead"?

"You're a bloody lummox, ya are, Perliss, an' that's a fact!"

"I said gimme room, an' I means *now*!" Pike snarled in response. "An' watch yer tongues, ya slimy lubbers, or I'll smash yer faces!"

Grumbling and resentful glares greeted Pike's arrogant ultimatum, but reluctantly the sullen seamen gave way, and the burly Pike claimed a prime spot at the rail.

Geoffry observed the angry exchange from above but refused to let it interfere for long with his attentive observation. To him, it represented just one more example of Pike Perliss's surly, obnoxious approach to all of life, typical of the actions they had come to expect from the nasty, consummate bully. It seemed to Geoffry that Pike actually went out of his way to be as totally disagreeable as possible. His nickname, "Pike," was rumored among the crew to have come from the fact that Perliss, in a fit of rage, had actually killed a fellow seaman aboard another vessel, using as a weapon the razor-pointed shaft of metal he was in the habit of carrying. Perliss had done nothing to discourage these rumors, and in fact appeared to relish his notorious, disorderly reputation.

"Bad blood" had developed early on between Pike Perliss and Geoffry Payne during the course of their voyage aboard the "Susan Constant." It had started late one evening when Geoffry caught Pike tormenting Billy Bascomb. Pike and Billy were assigned to stand watch on the fore deck, but Pike had soon devised a means of entertaining himself by harassing his shipmate. Billy, a small man, not too sure of himself and thus easily intimidated by the tyrannical Pike, was cowering before the brute, who kept jabbing at him with a stick.

"Crow like a rooster, boy! I sez, crow like a rooster! Ya wants ta warn them other ships out there that we's a' comin', don't ya, so they'll make way fer us? Ya wouldn't want us bangin' inta any o' 'em, now wouldja? So crow, boy, crow!"

Laughing uproariously at Billy's efforts, Pike kept prodding the little man, shouting, "Louder! Louder! Them blighters can't hear ya!"

"What's going on here?" Geoffry had demanded. Then, quickly assessing the situation, he had ordered, "Leave him alone, Pike!"

"Mind yer own bizness, Payne," Pike had growled. "The runt's on'y warnin' them other ships ta steer clear o' us, ya hear?" Again he guffawed as he continued to poke at the helpless Billy, who was still trying vainly to satisfy the demands of his tormentor.

"I said that's enough, Pike," Geoffry stated sharply. Grasping the stick, he wrenched it from Pike's grasp and hurled it overboard.

"Heyyy! Who d'ya think ya are, anyways? I'll teach ya to mess with Pike Perliss, I will, ya bloody blaggard!" bellowed the enraged bully. From behind his back, he whipped out his metal weapon, honed to a knife-sharp point at one end. Aiming the upraised shaft at Geoffry's face, he lunged forward, a fierce screech accompanying his attack. Only a swift, agile turn and side-step saved Geoffry from serious injury in the furious assault. As the screaming Pike stumbled past, Geoffry's right hand shot out, clenching Pike's wrist with an iron grip, spinning him to his knees.

Now the effects of years spent lifting and shaping cathedral stone came into play. Geoffry gradually tightened the pressure of his tenacious, unrelenting hold. A look of surprise flashed across Pike's eyes, followed by a grimace of pain that slowly creased his scarred face. As the powerful, vise-like grip continued to increase in intensity, the now-cringing Pike bellowed, "Leggo me, ya bloody ape. I said, *leggo*!"

"Drop your weapon, Pike, or I'll crush your wrist," came the uncompromising response.

Beads of sweat broke across Pike's swarthy face. Finally, only when he could tolerate the agony no longer, he blurted out, "A' right! A' right!" The metal rod clanged to the deck. "Ya don't gotta break a man's arm, does ya now?"

Still maintaining his hold, Geoffry seized the fallen weapon with his free hand and flung the shaft far out to sea. Only then did he release Pike's wrist.

"Heyyy, you can't do that! That there were *my* propity, it was!" Pike screamed, massaging his wrist as he stumbled to the railing and stared at the spot where the rod had disappeared. "Ya gots no right ta take a man's propity, ya ain't! I'm reportin' ya ta th' Cap'n, Payne, sure as I's borned!"

His brash attempt at bravado fell flat. Knowing he was beaten, Pike stood for a moment glowering at Geoffry. Then he turned and made his way aft, still muttering ominous threats over his shoulder.

"You jist wait, Payne! I ain't forgettin' this, I ain't! This here ain't th' last o' it, nosiree! I'll get ya yet, ya bloody beggar, jist wait'n' see!"

"You just leave Billy alone, you hear?" Geoffry yelled after the departing tyrant. Although he had managed to put a temporary end to Pike's tormenting of his little friend, Geoffry also knew instinctively that he had made a formidable, unforgiving foe.

"Wow! That's the first time I ever seen *anyone* stand up to ol' Pike, it is," Billy observed, admiration tingeing his voice. "I reckon the bloke's mighty happy no one else was around to see ya git the best of 'im, he is! He's just like all them cowards, though, ain't he ~ talking tough 'til someone challenges them?" A broad, appreciative smile illuminated Billy's face. "I surely do thank you, mate. I surely do." He reached up to pat the taller man's back. "You yanked ol' Pike up short, ya did, an' that's a fact."

"You're right, Billy, Pike's just like most bullies, picking on anyone they figure won't fight back. But when you call their bluff, they usually show that, deep down, they're nothing but a lot of bluster."

With a look akin to awe, Billy once more grinned up at his protector. "Well, thanks anyway, Geoffry," he said almost shyly. "You're a good mate, ya are!" With that, their bond of friendship had been sealed more securely than ever.

Chapter 3

▼

"There! Over there! I see it!" Geoffry cried suddenly, pointing to a shadowy outline only dimly visible in the morning mist. "Look! Over there, mates, just ahead on your left! It's land, sure enough."

Others on deck who had been distracted temporarily by Pike Perliss's arrogant display now turned to see where Geoffry was pointing. A moment of confusion ensued, filled with chaotic gesturing, shoving, and shouts of "Where? Where?" Then cheers burst from the assembled adventurers as they realized Geoffry was right! What they saw ahead really *was* land ~ the coveted "Promised Land!"

"Yeah, yeah! He's right! I see it! Look over there!"

"It's Virginia! We found 'er, we did, sure enough!"

"Hurrah! Hurrah! We found 'er!"

The undercurrent of disappointment at not being "first" to sight the long awaited goal gave way quickly to the sheer joy of knowing that they had indeed "made it," that they had actually *succeeded* in their quest. The fearsome ocean had been crossed! From now on, their fevered imaginations need accept no limits. Not only would they all soon be wealthy absolutely beyond belief, but each member of the expedition appeared on the verge of fulfilling his own grand personal destiny!

Even the ship's officers, their cabin boys tagging behind, as well as the aristocratic "gentlemen" who had joined the expedition but generally remained aloof and distant from the "commoners," now joined in the general melee on deck. All eyes strained to view what indisputably must be the gateway to almost instant wealth.

"That certainly *has* to be the Virginia coast, Lieutenant," Captain Newport remarked to the young officer at his side. "Tell the helmsmen to set a course north-by-northeast, parallel to the land, but not to get too close. And signal the other two ships of our intentions."

"Aye, aye, sir."

"And one more thing, Lieutenant. Locate the man who first spotted that shoreline. He's earned his reward, without a doubt!"

"Yes sir, Captain."

The wave of exuberance spread quickly to the "Discovery" and the "Godspeed," evidenced by shouts and cheers that echoed across the ocean's rising swells. Excited members of the crews on the two smaller vessels could be seen rushing boisterously about, waving their arms, pointing here, then there.

Meanwhile, inquiries as to who had given the "first alert" soon led the young officer to Geoffry, still aloft, observing everything from his perch in the rigging.

"You there, sailor. Come on down here! Captain Newport wants a word with you."

"Right away, sir." Geoffry scrambled down to the deck. He saluted the officer smartly.

"They tell me you're the bloke that first sighted the coast. Is that right?"

"Yes, sir. I believe so, sir."

"What's your name, sailor?"

"Geoffry Payne, sir. But I'm not really a sailor, sir. I'm just an indenture, working aboard to earn my way across."

"Payne, huh? Well, you've learned to salute better than a lot of the regulars, I'd say. Anyway, the Captain wants a word with you." He motioned for Geoffry to follow.

As they approached the fore deck where Captain Newport waited, Geoffry held back, keeping a respectful distance. The Lieutenant beckoned him forward.

"Captain Newport, sir, this here's Geoffry Payne. He's the one who sounded the first alert, sir."

Captain Newport turned toward Geoffry. Despite the Captain's customary air of aloofness and dignity, his clear, piercing blue eyes now calmly appraised the younger man. A hint of a smile crept over the stern, weathered face of the Captain, appearing to signal approval of the muscular frame, the erect posture of the man standing before him.

"So you're Geoffry Payne, are you?" The Captain extended his hand in a firm handshake, matched by that of Geoffry's own stone-callused hand. "Payne, Payne," he repeated the name as though it were somehow familiar. "I believe that's the name of a bookseller I came across in London. Thomas Payne. Had a collection of watercolor prints done by Governor John White, as I recall. You know, the leader of the 'Lost Colony' of Roanoke? This Payne wouldn't be a relative of yours perchance, now would he?"

"I don't believe so, sir. Not as far as I know, anyway."

"I don't recall you being one of our regular seamen, Payne."

"No, sir, I'm not. As I told the Lieutenant, sir, I'm an indenture, working my way over to the new settlement."

"Ah, an indenture, is it? Looks like you'll be able to work off the price of your passage rather quickly with those hands. What's your trade?"

"I was a stone mason, sir, from Salisbury, in Wiltshire County."

"Salisbury, you say? I know it well. I've worshipped in your magnificent cathedral there on several occasions. And what led you to leave such a fine little city for the risks of the unknown?"

Geoffry hesitated for a moment. "I guess I'm really not sure myself, sir. It's just that I knew that I didn't want to be a stone mason all my life. There are so many other things to try, so many places to see. I'm not sure *what* I'm looking for, really. I just know I want to experience something more than Salisbury, as fine a place as it is. So when one of your seamen, Billy Bascomb, told me about the London Company and their grand plans, I just couldn't resist." Geoffry halted and lowered his gaze, embarrassed by his burst of self-revelation. "Forgive me, Captain Newport, sir. I'm afraid I've blurted on way too long."

Captain Newport chuckled. "You remind me a good deal of myself at your age, young man. Couldn't wait to leave home for all those 'adventures' calling to me out there. Well, the Royal Navy provided me with plenty of those, I can tell you! But I've about had my fill of adventures by now. After we complete our mission here, I think I'll be ready to settle down to a nice, quiet country life for a change, maybe in some place like your Salisbury." A wistful, far-away look flickered across his solemn face. Then he continued: "Well, Payne, your sharp eyes stood you in good stead. When we start loading gold, just remember: the first big nugget is *yours*! And well-deserved it will be, too." He chuckled again. "Maybe after that you'll be ready to go back home to Salisbury yourself and settle down with some fine young lass, once you're rich."

"Thank you, sir, for your kindness," Geoffry replied softly, finishing with a snappy salute. He made his way back to the railing, unable to suppress a grin of pleasure at his great good fortune. He noticed that other seamen were looking at him with a new respect, a kind of awe ~ all except for Pike Perliss, whose disdainful sneer and hateful stare reflected only envy.

Among Geoffry's admirers was Billy Bascomb, who seemed genuinely delighted by his association with the new "celebrity." "By Gar, Geoffry, that was the Cap'n *himself* talkin' to ya, it was, laughin' and all, just like the two of you was old mates." He sidled up close, grinning as he patted Geoffry on the back. "Next thing ya know, he'll be askin' ya to take command o' one of these here ships, he will."

It was Geoffry's turn to chuckle. "I think we've had about enough disasters without adding to the lot by letting me run a ship, Billy. But the Captain *is* a right good sort, isn't he? I told him it was *you* that talked me into coming on this voyage."

"Did ya, now?" Billy sounded pleased. "Well, well! Then maybe it's *me* what'll get to be in command of a ship instead!" He laughed uproariously at his little joke.

Despite the initial elation at nearing their long-sought goal, everyone aboard gradually settled back to the tasks at hand. Following the Captain's orders, the small fleet shifted to a more north-easterly direction, tacking slowly, working its way closer to the dark shoreline now clearly visible in the distance. Captain Newport and his aide kept a close watch as details of the new land emerged in the morning light. Waves lashed and foamed over huge boulders, tangles of underbrush drifted in the swells, as did gnarled trees that appeared to have been uprooted by some passing storm.

Cautious, aware of the dangers in approaching an unfamiliar destination in such treacherous waters, Captain Newport directed the ships gradually toward a point of land protruding into the turbulent Atlantic. As the fleet drew ever nearer, even the usually disciplined and reserved senior officer couldn't hide his deep-felt emotions. Pounding a fist into his open palm, the Captain declared fervently, "*By God*, but it's good to finally be here! After all these weeks...." His voice trailed off.

"That it is, sir," his aide agreed quietly. "It surely is."

Both men fell silent, awed by the vistas unfolding before them. Forests of strange trees, trees taller and straighter than any they had ever seen, seemed to stretch to the horizon. Bright flowering bushes added brilliant patches of color to the scene. The lushness of the landscape revealed by the early morning sun was as unexpected as it was irresistible.

"Signal the other ships to prepare to halt and anchor, Lieutenant. We'll go ashore here."

"Aye, aye, sir!"

Orders were barked out to the seaman. Realization that their seemingly endless journey was about to conclude, that they were soon to set foot on solid land once more, led to renewed outbursts of cheering, back-slapping, and general jubilation as the sailors scurried about.

"Won't be long now, mates, and we'll all be rich as sin."

"Let's be gettin' ashore quick, so's we can get at some of that there gold!"

"Yeah! We've waited long enough for our share, and that's a fact!"

With the "Susan Constant," the "Godspeed," and the "Discovery" anchored safely off the point of land, near chaos ensued as the seamen all sought to cram into the small boats that would serve as their landing craft. It took the authoritative, clarion voice of Captain Newport to quiet the tumult.

"Order, men, *order!* We are explorers and settlers here, not a bloody London mob! Now ~ officers, permit six men per boat, no more! We'll go by lot, in a systematic fashion. We'll have no more of this infernal hubbub!"

Under the Captain's watchful eye, an element of discipline was restored and the boats began to ferry back and forth, discharging their human cargoes on the shore. Leading the way was Captain Newport himself in his own small skiff, accompanied by some of his junior officers.

At last, all one hundred and four adventurers ~ those who had survived the arduous journey ~ reached the relative safety of land, the land that for so long had been their great objective but had continued to elude them. Milling about, waiting impatiently, the men gazed in awe at the surroundings in which they now found themselves. A seemingly limitless forest stretched as far as the eye could see. The land was ablaze with colorful spring blossoms. Wild grapes and berries abounded everywhere, and they caught occasional glimpses of animals moving stealthily through the shadows in the woods. Unfamiliar birds flitted noisily amongst the arching tree branches.

Once again Captain Newport called for order. "It is only fitting, on this momentous occasion, that we offer a prayer of thanksgiving to Divine Providence for protection during our journey," he informed them. As the men quieted, the Captain bowed his head: "Almighty God, we thank you for granting us safe passage to these alien shores. We now ask your blessing and guidance upon this sacred undertaking, as well as your mercy for those sixteen souls who perished during our passage and were buried at sea. Amen."

A chorus of rough "Amens" echoed as the Captain concluded. But Captain Newport was not yet ready to turn the men loose to pursue their *true* interest ~ the search for gold. He went on: "Now, men, we have one more vital item of business to conclude. You see this small wooden chest I'm holding? This was given to me by the directors of the London Company before we sailed. In it are the names of those of our number selected by the directors to serve as the Council of Virginia, the governing body for the colony we propose to establish here. It is time now to open the chest and determine who will be in charge here, who will lead our grand endeavor."

Murmurs of anticipation spread through the assembled group. Seamen, indentures, artisans, "gentlemen" ~ *all* seemed curious to know who would set and enforce the rules of conduct under which the group would live from now on. All appeared aware of the importance of wise leadership in this otherwise anarchic wilderness.

Captain Newport withdrew the list from the small chest, scanned the names briefly, then handed it to his Lieutenant to read aloud. The Lieutenant cleared his throat, slowly surveying his waiting audience to emphasize the significance of what they were about to hear. Then in a firm voice he read the first name.

"First on the list is our very own Captain Newport." The announcement brought a round of enthusiastic cheers and "huzzahs," as well as a pleased look from the Captain.

Waiting for the group to quiet down again, the Lieutenant went on: "Next, we have Captain John Ratcliffe of the 'Discovery,' and Captain Bartholomew Gosnold of the 'Godspeed.'"

Once more shouts of approval interrupted, seeming to signify endorsement of these selections as well. Finally the officer was able to continue. "The others listed are: Mr. Edward Maria Wingfield, an ex-soldier, as you may know, and one of our investors; Mr. George Kendall and Mr. John Martin, both experienced seafaring gentlemen; and last on the list is the name of Captain John Smith."

Chapter 4

▼

Gasps of surprise, along with mutterings of intense disapproval, greeted the announcement of John Smith's appointment to the Council of Virginia. The response from the "gentlemen" was especially negative. As Geoffry glanced around, observing their reactions, he saw heads shake in disbelief and heard loud undercurrents of angry grumbling.

"Not *that* liar, for God's sake!"

"I say, we should've hanged the blighter while we had the chance."

Geoffry glanced over to where Smith was standing, somewhat apart from the group, a slight smile playing on his face.

While Geoffry had not had any personal dealings with the short, bearded individual who styled himself "Captain John Smith," he nonetheless remembered vividly the acrimony surrounding many of the Captain's actions during their lengthy voyage. What he knew about Smith on a personal level Geoffry had gleaned mostly from conversations with Billy Bascomb, who appeared to have an uncanny knack for obtaining surreptitious bits of information about almost everyone.

Seeing Captain Smith on one occasion standing at the prow of the "Susan Constant," his gaze carrying to distant horizons, Billy had nudged Geoffry and informed him in a muted voice, "Now *there's* a gentleman what I can respect, I tell ya. Why, he's had more adventures in his life than any man I ever heard tell of, an' that's a fact."

"What do you mean, 'adventures'"?

"Oh, it just seems like he's been 'bout ever'wheres and done 'bout ever'thin' there is to do in this whole wide *world*, it does. Leastwise to hear *him* tell it, he surely has."

"How do you know all this about him, Billy?"

Billy grinned a bit sheepishly, but the twinkle in his eyes belied any real embarrassment. "Oh, I learned it accidental-like, I guess ya could say."

"How was that, Billy? Come on, you can tell your old mate, can't you?"

Billy sidled closer, again reverting to his best conspiratorial tone. "Well, it happened like this, mate. It was my turn to stand watch on the fo'castle one night, it was. It was a dark night, see, and nothin' special was happenin', so I decided to settle down against a bulkhead for a little rest, I did. But I must've dozed off, like ~ just for a minute, ya understand ~ 'cause pretty soon I heard these here voices, not far away. Turns out it was Cap'n Smith talkin' with some other feller I couldn't make out. Anyway, Cap'n Smith had a bottle with him, he did, and the two of 'em was a'nippin' away, and they kept gettin' louder and louder with their talk. They never even knowed I was there, nosiree. That's when I heard 'bout all his adventures."

Billy paused for a moment, waiting to be urged on by a curious Geoffry.

"And just what *were* those 'adventures', Billy? Tell me about them."

"Well, it seems to me like that there Cap'n Smith is a right gen-u-ine hero, he is. I heard him go on and on, tellin' that other feller about all them fancy places what he's been at, and how he killed them Turks, and all. He's a real hero, sure enough."

"Did you say he killed some *Turks?*"

"Yep. Three of 'em. Killed 'em plumb dead, he did."

"Come on, Billy, stop dragging everything out so long. Just tell me what happened."

"Well, accordin' to Cap'n Smith, he took up soldierin' right early on, he did, when he was but a mere lad o' sixteen. Then he went to sea for a while, and later he joined up with the Austrian Army, if ya can imagine. That's when he fought them Turks. Killed three o' their best fighters in hand-to-hand combat, he did, right there in front o' both armies. Used only his pistol and a lance and a axe. Cut their heads clean off! And that's why he was made a Cap'n, and was give a horse and a coat o' arms what's got three Turk heads on it, an' all. But that there ain't the end of it. Nosiree!"

Knowing he had a rapt listener, Billy waited, appearing to enjoy tantalizing Geoffry with his tale. Again he was urged to get on with the story.

"Well, next time he fought against them Turks, Cap'n Smith was wounded, he was, and captured, too. But you'd never, ever guess what happened after that, you wouldn't! Never in a million years!"

"Billy!"

"I *knew* you couldn't guess it, mate! Well, he was sold as a slave, he was. What do ya think o' that?"

"Sold as a *slave?* Who to, for Heaven's sake?"

"Sold to a Turkish Pasha, he was. And then this here Pasha sent him right on to Con-stan-ti-nople. Sent him there as a present, he did, for his sweetheart."

"Come on, Billy! You're making all of this up, aren't you?"

"No I ain't, mate, no I ain't! It's the God's truth, just like Cap'n Smith told it to that other feller. Honest it is!" Billy's sincerity was strong enough to convince Geoffry that he was indeed only repeating what he had heard.

"Then how did Smith get away?"

"Oh, that there's the best part, it is! Ya see, when the Pasha's sweetheart got this here present of a handsome British soldier, she just couldn't resist 'im, she couldn't! Nosiree! Fell head-over-heels in love with 'im, she did. Now what do ya think of *that?*"

"Billy! Now I *know* you're making all this up!"

"No I ain't, mate! I *ain't!* Swear to God! It's azzactly like Cap'n Smith told it, it is! And you know what happened next? Well, after Cap'n Smith had romanced this here Turkish gal for a while ~ and she was quite a beauty, too, to hear him tell it ~ she sent 'im off to her brother, she did. Wanted 'im trained proper for 'imperial service,' she says, so he'd always be right available. Whoo-ee! But they didn't know who they was dealin' with, they didn't. Not on your life!"

"Billy, just tell…"

"Hah! Got ya curious now, ain't I? Well, just remember, *I'm* the only one what knows how it all comes out, so ya gotta listen to it *my* way." He grinned at the look of impatient resignation on Geoffry's face before he went on.

"Well, that's how Cap'n Smith come to kill one more o' them Turks, it is. Killed that girl's brother, he did, killed 'im and then escaped. Traveled up into Rooshia, where he was helped out by *another* beautiful lady, o' course. This one sent 'im on to Poland, but sure enough, he finally got clean away. Even went down to Afriker before gettin' back home to England, he did. And now, after all o' them adventures ~ there he stands," Billy concluded.

Geoffry had to admit a newly aroused interest in the mysterious Captain John Smith. He wasn't sure what to make of Billy's extravagant recitation. Still, the story was so far-fetched, so bizarre that Geoffry was convinced Billy's rather limited imagination alone could never have conjured up such an incredible tale. At least it did cast the somber Captain in a new light.

Geoffry knew only too well that Captain Smith was currently viewed with antagonism by many of his fellow voyagers. During the long months at sea, the Captain had often been openly critical of many of the ship's officers. But he had reserved his *deepest* disdain for those passengers who classed themselves as "gentlemen." This latter group appeared to feel that their "elevated station" in English society entitled them to special privileges and treatment, no matter where they were or what the circumstances. Smith's brusque, contemptuous attitude toward these self-exalted "elitists" had led to frequent clashes, until finally the querulous Captain had been placed under arrest and clapped into chains.

In fact, Geoffry recalled further what had followed when their little fleet first came to the island of Martinique in the West Indies. Some of Smith's opponents proceeded to build a gallows on the island, with the intention of hanging the quarrelsome Captain. Fortunately for Smith, Captain Newport intervened. As Smith had later observed wryly regarding the gallows: "I could not be persuaded to *use* them!"

But now, with Smith legally established as a member of the ruling Council of Virginia in spite of all objections from the "gentlemen," Captain Newport informed the prospective settlers that it was time to get down to the business at hand: choosing a site for their planned settlement. A small advance party was selected, made up of both "gentlemen" and military men. Their instructions were to explore the surrounding area, but also to go farther inland, if possible, searching for a spot suitable for *permanent* colonization ~ one with adequate water and land capable of cultivation.

Muttered grumbling greeted this further delay in allowing the gold-seekers to pursue their *true* interest.

"Why ain't we settlin' down right *here*?"

"Yeah, this is *Virginia*, ain't it? Why can't we just go ahead and start lookin' for our gold?"

It was Billy Bascomb who provided an explanation: "The first mate is sayin' that Cap'n Newport wants us to settle further *in*, further away from the coast. Cap'n's afraid that if we stays out on this here cape, right in plain sight, some bloody Spanish raider'll come by and treat us to some broadsides, sure enough. He figures we'll be safer if we moves on *in* a ways, he does." Despite their impatience, a general consensus emerged that the Captain's plan made "good sense."

When the exploration party returned the next day, they reported coming upon the mouth of a great river not too far distant from where the group was currently camped. After brief consultation, members of the Council of Virginia reached their decision: they would all prepare to move on, to establish their settlement farther inland, somewhere less vulnerable to Spanish attack than the exposed cape upon which they had landed.

Before re-boarding began, however, Captain Newport ordered the erection of a large cross to mark the spot of their first landing. While some of the men fashioned a crude cross by lashing together at right angles the trunks of two small trees they had cut down, Geoffry and Billy Bascomb busied themselves digging a hole at the prescribed location. Geoffry next picked up the assembled cross and set it into the newly dug hole, shrugging off offers of assistance. While he held the cross in place, others packed dirt firmly around it to hold it upright. With their task completed, the little group stepped back to a respectful distance.

"Good job, men," commended Captain Newport, bringing smiles to the faces of the work party. "Now, it seems only fitting that we again give thanks to Almighty God for bringing us safely to these shores. And it is also fitting that we select an appropriate *name* for this promontory that marks the successful ending to our difficult journey. I've been giving this some thought, and I believe I may have come up with the proper solution. So ~ I hereby decree that this point of land shall henceforth be known as Cape Henry, named in honor of the eldest son of our Sovereign Majesty, King James of England."

Spontaneous cheers erupted from the assembled adventurers. Then, still in high spirits, laughing and bantering amongst themselves, the travelers gathered up their belongings and straggled back on board.

With everyone accounted for, the three ships began to work their way slowly westward. Leading the way as usual was the "Susan Constant," with Captain Newport on the fore deck accompanied by his junior officers. One of these men, the young Lieutenant, approached the Captain, holding a crude map. "According to these old drawings by Sir Walter Raleigh, sir, we now appear to be in the waters of what he called Chesapeake Bay."

Captain Newport briefly studied the map, then nodded in agreement.

"I think you're right, Lieutenant. And back here, then," he pointed to a spot on the map, "this must be the area where the exploring party found that river. It can't be much farther."

Gliding almost noiselessly through the placid bay, the fleet soon approached what appeared to be the mouth of a broad river. As the officers exclaimed over this new geographic feature, the Lieutenant remained silent, eyes narrowed, deep in thought. Finally he turned to Captain Newport and posed a question with enormous hidden potential.

"That river looks big enough to lead a long way into the Virginia interior, doesn't it, Captain?"

"That it does," Captain Newport concurred. "Seems like it could be a pretty good water route for trade, and all."

But the Lieutenant had a much grander vision in mind. In a quiet voice, he went on: "Do you suppose, sir, it could be that water route that goes all the way to the *Pacific?* The one we were told to find?"

Captain Newport looked sharply at the young officer, momentarily taken aback. Then, apparently grasping the truly immense significance of the question, he began to nod enthusiastically. "You know, it just could *be,* Lieutenant, though it appears a bit narrow for such a grand passageway. Still, if it is…" ~ his voice took on a whole new tone of excitement ~ "if it *is* indeed the route explorers have been searching for all these years, why, think of the *riches* that lie just beyond, in the Orient!"

"Not only riches, sir, but control of that passageway would allow England to dominate the entire *sea route,*" rejoined the aide. "It's like that clergyman Richard Hakluyt wrote in his pamphlet. We could build a fort at the entrance, and then we could force anyone who goes through to pay us a toll."

"Aye, that we could." The Captain remained silent for a time, deep in thought. At last he looked up and called for all of his officers to gather around as he made his announcement. "Since this may well be a most vital future waterway, it should bear a truly significant name: that of our esteemed Sovereign. We'll call this river the *James* River, named after our good King James himself."

"Does that mean that this is where we'll set up our permanent base, sir?" asked the first mate.

Again the Captain pondered the question before stating his decision: "No, I think a settlement here would still be too vulnerable, still too easy for the Spanish coming up from the south to attack. We'll move upstream a ways and get a better look at the surroundings."

Entering the mouth of the river, the three ships began to work their way slowly against its languid current. The new course of action led once more to objections from the anxious seamen and adventurers.

"You mean we *still* ain't stoppin'? Where we goin' to, anyways?"

"Who knows? But it's high time we was gettin' off this here tub, if'n ya asks me."

"Can't find no gold from here, that's for sure!"

Still the small ships continued to push upstream. Finally, about thirty miles inland from the mouth of what they now called the "James River," they approached a peninsula jutting sharply out into the stream. The fleet slowed to permit closer assessment of the terrain. Finally word came from Captain Newport: "Send two sailors from each ship ashore with lines. We'll tie up to those trees over there for now. Everyone stays on board until some of us can determine the lay of the land."

More uneasy hours passed, until at last the small advance party returned. Captain Newport came back aboard the "Susan Constant" to make the dramatic announcement: *"This is it,* men! This is where we disembark! This is where we shall establish the settlement that will provide England a foothold in this New World. *Long live King James!"*

Chapter 5

▼

Captain Newport's welcome words brought a rousing chorus of "huzzahs" and cheers that echoed across the quiet river valley, startling bright-colored birds into hasty flight. Geoffry, like every other passenger who had survived to this point, knew he should consider himself extremely fortunate. Now at last they were about to set foot on what would ever after be called "English soil" ~ though it was actually the soil of a world totally *unknown* to the English only a few generations earlier. Here indeed was the "Promised Land," the land of dreams, a land filled with unbounded golden allure.

Geoffry watched the eager, impatient assemblage clamber noisily over the sides of the ships and into small boats that ferried them to the nearby shore. As he surveyed the group, he couldn't help but marvel at its diversity and disparity. Even more, it was hard to imagine a less likely collection of individuals to hazard such a grandiose venture.

They totaled one hundred and four human souls, and Billy Bascomb had proved to be an irrepressible source of information regarding their personal lives. How he managed to ferret out details of the varied backgrounds that were represented remained a mystery, yet he was only too happy to impress Geoffry whenever possible with his newly discovered knowledge.

He had first broached the subject as they chatted one day during their long voyage: "Did you know that we is in the proud company of an outstanding group o' *'gentlemen,'* mate? Did ya, now?"

"What do you mean, Billy?"

"Why, our fella passengers, o' course! Who else? Know what the first mate told me, now do ya?"

"Of course I don't, Billy. But I'll bet you'll be happy to fill me in, won't you?"

"Well, it *is* pretty special information, it is. But seein' as how you're my mate, an' all…" The sentence trailed off, but the light in Billy's eyes and his playful grin betrayed his eagerness to share what he knew.

Geoffry responded with a grin of his own. "Go ahead and tell me, Billy. Or would you like me to beg a little first?"

"Alright, I'll tell ya! Accordin' to the first mate, 'most a third o' the folks that's joined up with our 'noble expedition' ain't nothin' less than regular 'gentlemen'. Yessir, '*gentlemen*'! At least that's how they lists themselves on the manifest, he says. 'Gentlemen,' without givin' any other occupation. They's 'gentlemen', says they, an' should be treated as such! Humph! Have ya ever heard such stupid arrogance? Now, have ya?"

"Don't they list any skills, or trades they might know, or whether they were successful businessmen or anything?"

"Nosiree, they surely don't. They seems to feel just bein' 'gentlemen' should be good enough for *anyone*, they does. Blimey! Of all the high-falutin' airs!"

"Well, do they have large fortunes, then? Or are they investors in the London Company? Maybe that's why they…"

Billy cut him off. "Oh sure, a few o' them has money or land or is investors, I reckon. But I tell ya, most of 'em has flat *lost* their fortunes, or is just barely hangin' on. They see this here Virginia as a way to get back that what they once had, they do. And maybe more!" Billy paused, then finished with a sarcastic chuckle: "But they surely ain't lost none o' their high-and-mighty ways, though, has they? Nosiree, that they ain't!"

"What will they do in the new settlement then, do you suppose?" Geoffry wondered. "What do 'gentlemen' *do*, anyway?"

Billy answered with a harsh laugh. "Oh, they'll expect ever'one to wait on 'em hand and foot, they will, just like they's used to back home. You wait and see! Once a gentleman, always a gentleman, they seems to think." He turned away in disgust, calling back, "What a bunch o' worthless sods!"

Now, as Geoffry surveyed the aloof, pompous gathering, all elegantly attired, talking only amongst themselves and generally ignoring the rest of the group, he couldn't help but agree with Billy's assessment. Their only acknowledgement of so much as the *existence* of anyone else was to call out an occasional preemptory demand to one of their servants huddled close by. Geoffry wondered anew just what contributions they could possibly make, if any, to the success of this great venture. He did not feel reassured.

Those servants and stewards for the "gentlemen" comprised a second class in the make-up of the settlers. Geoffry had observed these individuals at their tasks during the long weeks aboard the "Susan Constant," waiting compliantly on masters who insisted on maintaining all of the trappings of "home" despite the arduous conditions of travel. The submissive demeanor, the ingratiating servility demonstrated by these attendants was repugnant to Geoffry's democratic sensibilities, though he knew only too well that this was, and had long been, part of the "proper English order." As with their masters, the background and training of these servants had prepared them to fulfill a particular role in a well-ordered society. But he feared they would be woefully unprepared and ill-equipped for the future they were now facing in this stark wilderness.

The remainder of the group ~ less than half the total, Geoffry estimated ~ had signed on as "laborers," just as he had himself. He had learned from conversations aboard ship that this group represented a rather broad assortment of both backgrounds and skills. Among these were several men listed as "goldsmiths" and "refiners," evidently recruited to work the precious metals everyone seemed absolutely certain they would soon find. But Geoffry had also come across representatives of more unique trades: "glassblowers," "silk-raisers," and "wine makers." Surprised to find practitioners of these somewhat exotic occupations heading for a strange, wild land, he had questioned them: "Exactly how do you plan to *utilize* your special skills out there in the wilderness of Virginia?"

"Oh, it won't be a wilderness for long," he had been assured. "You just wait and see. We'll have those savages tamed in no time. We'll introduce them to the ways of a proper English civilization, and the next thing you know they'll be setting up trade with our settlements, seeing as how they'll be needing all of our products. It's just one more way the London Company plans to get returns on its investment, don't you know."

Geoffry remained skeptical. And yet, he had to admit, in a way they were *all* gambling their futures in hopes of making great financial gain. Personally, he would be required to promote the welfare of the London Company for the next seven years. Like many of his fellow laborers, he was an "indenture." Unable to raise the money to pay for his passage to Virginia, he had agreed to provide his *labor* to the Company for that length of time as an "indentured servant" in exchange for the price of transit. *Seven years!* Still, secretly Geoffry was convinced that, through his own diligent efforts, he would quickly find the plentiful gold that had attracted them all and would become rich enough to "pay off" his indenture, even with its exorbitant interest rates. Then he would be *free* ~ free to pursue his *own* interests and well-being.

The voice of Captain Newport broke the train of Geoffry's thoughts. Now that the entire party had finally reached land safely, they were milling about, exclaiming over the wonders of their new environment. The Captain called for attention. Then, drawing his magnificently-wrought saber from its jewel-encrusted scabbard, he raised the weapon aloft at arms length. In a strong voice, he proclaimed, "On this 14th day of May, in the year of our Lord one thousand six hundred and seven, I hereby lay claim to this land in the name of His Royal Highness King James of England and his successors, forever! Be it also known by all men everywhere that this land shall henceforth be named *Virginia*, in honor of Her Majesty our dear departed Queen Elizabeth. Long live the King!"

From where they were watching in the shade of two brushy trees near the edge of the small clearing, Billy Bascomb and Geoffry Payne joined in the hearty cheering. There was a general aura of celebration, an understandable surge of joy and pride to be standing once again upon "English soil." Adding to this euphoric spirit, Geoffry experienced an almost mystical perception that indeed this truly *was* a "new beginning," that somehow his personal world would never again be quite the same.

But there was to be little time for such idle reflection. Captain Newport's next words were stern: "All right, men, it's time for everyone to get to work. I want the remaining goods from all three ships unloaded. Stack everything right over there. Be careful! We'll need every ounce of those supplies, you can be sure. Don't spoil anything by letting it get wet."

For the rest of the day, every available laborer and many of the "servants" toiled diligently, bringing crate after crate, load after load, from the ships to the designated location. As they made their way back and forth between ship and shore, Geoffry could not help but notice with some disgust the role that the "gentlemen" had assigned to themselves. They refused to participate in the work in any way. Rather, they gathered in the shade of a stately old cypress, laughing, talking, sipping their port or sherry from crystal goblets or savoring their steins of beer. Whenever a personal need arose, they called impatiently for their servants or stewards to fulfill their wishes. Only when their every desire had been attended to were the servants dismissed with an aristocratic wave of a gloved hand and permitted to return to assist with the unloading. Captain Newport seemed reluctant to interfere or to impose any type of discipline upon the group, in apparent deference to their "elevated" status.

Billy Bascomb, on the other hand, was not at all hesitant to voice his opinion, if only to Geoffry: "Just look at those lazy clods, will you now, mate? Carryin' on for all the world like they was still at one o' their fancy clubs back in ol' London or somethin'. I swear, I hope they *all* starves to death, I do! And good riddance!"

Geoffry laughed, at least partially in agreement with Billy's sentiments. He only hoped that he and Billy would find the riches they were seeking without undue delay so that they could quickly return home, away from such frivolous "parasites."

Continuing with their duties, the two returned to the "Susan Constant." As they descended the companionway to the ship's hold, they came unexpectedly upon Pike Perliss, a bottle of wine clutched firmly in one hand while he attempted to hide another bottle under his jacket. Before him lay a partially opened crate from which the wine had obviously been taken.

"Hey, Perliss, what's going on here?" Geoffry called out.

Surprised by the sudden challenge, Pike Perliss nearly dropped the bottle he was trying to conceal. A look of fear flashed briefly across his furtive features. When he recognized who had discovered him, however, the fear was replaced by a dark scowl.

"Oh, it's *you*, is it, Payne?" he snarled. "Allus innerferin,' ain't ya? Well, it's none 'o yer bizness *what* I'm a'doin,' it ain't!" But seeming to realize the danger of being caught pilfering supplies, he blurted out, "If ya gotta know, this here crate busted open whilst I was a'movin' it, it did, an' some o' th' bottles was spillin' out, so's I was jist puttin' 'em back. Tha's th' truth! Tha's azzackly what'uz happenin.' I was jist puttin' 'em back! So don't go runnin' off ta tattle ta th' Cap'n er nothin,' ya hear? If'n ya does, ol' Pike'll make ya good an' sorry, he will." As if for emphasis, he added, "An' I ain't fergot how ya threwed away my pike, neither, I ain't!"

"You don't scare us with all your bluster, Pike," Geoffry retorted. "Just get back to your job and stay out of our way!" With that, he and Billy returned to their tasks, leaving the grumbling Pike Perliss to his own devices.

"Blimey, but he's a right sneaky one, ain't he now?" Billy observed when they were out of earshot. "Sooner or later, he's gonna be trouble, just mark my words, mate. That Pike's downright *mean*, he is, through an' through."

"You're absolutely right, Billy," Geoffry agreed. "But we can't let him intimidate us either, no matter *what* he does! I guess we'll just have to be extra careful and keep an eye out for him, as best we can."

Chapter 6

▼

With their labors completed, the men were finally given leave to go about making their own preparations for spending the night. Geoffry and Billy wandered back to where they had waited earlier, at the edge of the little clearing.

"Hey, mate, why don't we just bunk down right here, under these here scrubby trees?" Billy asked.

"Seems as good a place as any," Geoffry replied. "Not much shelter from rain or cold, though."

"Oh, we'll get 'round to buildin' us a proper shelter soon enough. Just be happy it's springtime, 'stead o' the middle o' winter, right?"

"You bet! Shouldn't have much trouble finding plenty of timber and stuff around here to build us a better place, should we? Something more suitable. All it'll take is some hard work."

"Yeah, seems like 'bout *everthin'* here takes a lot of hard work, don't it, mate? But what do ya say we see 'bout gettin' us somethin' to eat first? Looks like we're on our own from now on, it does. Just hope there's enough of them supplies left to last awhile."

"That *could* be a serious problem, I'm afraid," Geoffry mused. "Didn't seem like there was all that much stuff left when we unloaded the ships, did it? But I'm sure the Captain and the Council will figure it all out."

As he and Billy continued setting up their simple temporary campsite, after first building a small fire to heat water for tea, Geoffry's mind kept playing back over the question of supplies. He knew they had loaded adequate quantities while the ships were docked back in London, but that had been a very long time ago. A great deal had transpired in the meantime.

The two men busied themselves with the tasks necessary for preparing a place to spend the night. But Geoffry's thoughts were elsewhere. His concern over supplies led to a meandering mental review of the entire series of incredible events that had brought them finally to this point at this time, to this strange new place, this "new beginning."

The little fleet had set out from Blackwell, near London, he recalled, back on December 20th of the previous year, 1606, almost five months before. Bad luck had stalked the expedition almost from the beginning. For six weeks, severe storms and unseasonable weather held them off the coast of Kent. It wasn't until February of 1607 that the winds had finally shifted, enabling their three small ships to get underway.

The delay had led naturally to consumption of a sizeable portion of the provisions set aside not only for utilization during their journey but also to provide sustenance until they could establish their settlement. Yet, when the weather improved at last, Captain Newport, impatient at the forced delay, had *refused* to return to port to replenish their lost stores. Instead, he determined to head for Virginia at once.

Then, for reasons not understood by the adventurers ~ who were, after all, completely at the mercy of the ships' Captains and the London Company's orders ~ the route chosen to reach Virginia proved to be a long, circuitous one. Rather than steer directly across the stormy North Atlantic, the decision had been made to have the little fleet follow the longer but supposedly safer route first pioneered by Columbus.

Thus Geoffry remembered vividly the many long, dreary days and nights aboard the "Susan Constant" as the three ships proceeded slowly out of the Channel, south along the coast of France, down past the coasts of Spain and northern Africa to the Canary Islands. Only then, after refilling their water casks, had they turned westward for the difficult crossing to the West Indies.

Now, as he and Billy busied themselves with preparations for settling in, Geoffry's mind drifted back to the nightmarish hardships of that particular leg of the journey. He called out to his companion:

"Hey, Billy, having our feet on solid ground again sure beats what it took to get here, doesn't it?"

"Don't be remindin' me, mate," Billy groaned. "I just hopes most o' my sailin' days is over and done for, an' that's a fact!"

"Remember how sick we both got when that storm caught us half-way across from the Canaries?"

"I *told* ya, don't be remindin' me! We was so sick we'da had to get better a'fore we could *die,* we was, an' that's the truth! I was plumb certain we was *all* headin' straight down to Davy Jones's locker, I was! Right down into the briney deep, and before we'd even had our chance to get rich an' all."

"Yeah, I guess we were pretty lucky just to survive, alright. Those ships of ours were pretty small to be taking on such a big ocean!"

"That they was, mate, that they surely was! I reckon we oughta at least be happy we was on the *biggest* one, bad as it was."

Geoffry continued: "And remember when we finally sighted that little island ~ Martinique, I think it was? It sure looked like heaven, didn't it?"

"Oh yeah, that it truly did," Billy agreed with a laugh. "And we got to stay there for three whole weeks, we did, eatin' fresh fruit and tradin' stuff and tryin' to get friendly with them native gals an' all." He laughed again. "Tell the truth mate, I wouldn't o' minded stayin' right there *permanent* like, an' hang the gold!"

"But when we finally *did* go on again, we had us another good time on that island off Puerto Rico, too. Remember that one?"

"Yeah, 'course I do. You mean the one what had 'bout a million birds on it, don't ya, and we went and stole us all them bird's eggs?" Billy chuckled happily at the recollection.

"Right! Came near filling two of our little boats with 'em. Even had enough to share with the other two ships!"

"That we did, mate, that we did." Billy grinned in remembrance. "That was somethin,' it was, alright. Surely give us a nice change from eatin' hardtack and salt fish and barley gruel, I tell ya!"

He paused for a bit as though in reverie, then blurted out, "Blimey, mate, we's had us some real fine esperiences together, ain't we now?'

Geoffry chuckled at Billy's enthusiasm, and for a while both men returned to the tasks at hand. After some minutes of quiet reflection, however, Billy sidled closer and in an unusually subdued tone confided, "But can I tell you somethin' private-like, mate, seein' as how you ain't a blabber-mouth an' all? Ya know what scared me the *most* back there when the goin' was gettin' so rough an' all, and it looked like we was never gonna make it, no ways?" He hesitated, seeming reluctant to reveal his personal thoughts.

"What's that, Billy?" Geoffry encouraged.

In a hushed voice, Billy told him, "What *really* scared me was, I was afraid I was prob'ly never *ever* gonna get back home again to see my Mum! That's a fact, mate! I just wanted to see my ol' Mum again."

Surprised at Billy's unusual show of emotion, Geoffry remained silent for a time, continuing to prepare their meager meal. At last he said quietly, "Tell me about your Mum, Billy."

Billy looked closely at his friend, a grateful smile lighting his face as though thankful that his sentimental revelation had been taken seriously and not as a sign of being a "sissy." "She's all I got in this whole world, she is, mate! She may not be much by the standards o' some o' them 'gentlemen' over there, I reckon, but to me she's always been a gen-u-ine angel!" He paused before going on. "Tell the truth, mate, she's the mainest reason why I joined up on this here adventure, she is."

"Oh? How's that, Billy?"

"Well, she's the reason I'm wantin' to get rich, don't ya see? Her life's always been real hard, it has, especially after my Pa up and died from the consumption. Pa worked in the coal mines, ya know, and it was a tough way to make a livin,' an that's the truth! Even when he started gettin' sickly an' all, he just kept right on a' goin,' he did, 'til he jist *couldn't* go no more. After that, things got even worse for Mum, tryin' to take care o' both me and her all by herself. But she never complained, never said nothin.' Just kept on a'workin' and a'strugglin,' she did." After a moment of quiet, Billy added, "She deserves better'n that, she does, mate. And I aims to see she gets it!"

"She sounds like a great Mum, Billy. Reminds me some of my own Mum, though life always seemed to be a lot easier for her. And you know what? I've got to admit that I really miss *my* Mum, too ~ an awful lot! Sometimes I get so homesick to be back in good old Salisbury I can hardly stand it!"

Tears glistened in Billy's eyes as he looked up at his friend. "Thanks for understandin', Geoffry, and for not laughin'. You're truly a good mate, ya are, an' that's a fact!"

Geoffry patted the little man on the back and handed him a plate of food, not trusting himself to speak for fear that his *own* emotions would get the best of him. They finished their skimpy meal in silence, both seeming to realize unconsciously that, as a result of their exchange, the bond of friendship had once more been deepened and strengthened.

The excitement of their new surroundings, plus the grandiose *improbability* of the entire venture, made it difficult for both men to settle down for the night. Having shaken out their blankets and patted them into crude bedrolls, they continued chatting amiably until finally overtaken by exhaustion brought on by the long day's exertions.

As the first light of a new day dawned, it brought a flurry of activity throughout the encampment. Men barely took time to eat, and none at all to prepare for the duties of the day. Rather, they spread out rapidly amongst the trees, vigorously wielding shovels, picks, adzes, or even sharpened sticks in frantic efforts to dig into the sandy soil of the peninsula, searching for the precious metal all seemed certain lay just beneath its surface. Cries of, "Hey, that there's my spot!" or "Get away from here! I was here first!" mingled with a general hubbub of curses and laughter.

"Will you look at that, mate?" Billy muttered as he rolled over and raised himself on one elbow, watching the melee. "Looks like they's plumb turned into a bunch o' lunatics, don't it now?"

Geoffry chuckled. "Well, shall we join them, or do you want to eat first? Maybe there won't be anything left if we wait too long."

Billy glanced sharply at his companion, trying to determine whether the remark was meant seriously. Geoffry's irrepressible grin gave the answer.

"I reckon ya agrees with me, then, don't ya, mate? Besides, there really ain't *no* amount o' gold what's more important than good old food, is there now?"

They set about preparing tea, along with a few scanty provisions, and had almost finished their morning repast when a stern, booming voice broke abruptly into the hectic activity all around them. Captain Newport had appeared on the scene.

"What in God's name is going *on* here?" the Captain bellowed. "Have you all gone *mad*? Get over here *right now*, the lot of you, and bring those tools with you, *you hear?*"

The startled "prospectors," dismayed at yet another delay in their quest for wealth but nonetheless fearful of the Captain's forceful command, hurried to gather around the irate officer. Scattered grumbling was quickly quieted as he demanded: "What's the meaning of all this? Don't you men realize we have more *important* things to do than run around digging *holes* in the ground? Our very *survival* depends upon working together cooperatively, in an orderly and organized fashion." He paused, his fierce, searching stare sweeping the assemblage.

From somewhere near the rear of the group came the question: "But *why*, Cap'n? We come here to get rich, didn't we? Let's find our gold, so's we can all get on back home!" The remark brought nods of assent, mingled with mumbled expressions of agreement.

Captain Newport remained uncompromising. *"Quiet, all* of you!" he thundered. "Remember, every person here is under command of the London Company and the Council of Virginia, and therefore will act *only* in accordance with their wishes and for their best interests. *Is that clear?*"

The disappointed gold-seekers waited in subdued silence for further direction.

"Now, this is the manner in which we will proceed: First and foremost, we must insure the safety of the expedition. Accordingly, we shall begin immediately to construct fortifications for protection against attack from the natives. To oversee construction, I am placing in charge Captain John Smith."

Once again, the name of the controversial Captain brought grumbles of protest:

"Not *that* confounded braggart!"

"Not Smith, for God's sake!"

"*Silence!*" commanded Captain Newport. "You *will* obey the orders of Captain Smith, and you *will* put forth your best efforts to construct the necessary bastion, James Fort. It is imperative! *Does everyone understand?*" He stared defiantly at his unhappy audience for a moment, then turned on his heel and strode back to his tent.

Captain John Smith, who had been standing at a respectful distance behind Captain Newport, now stepped forward. Slowly, intently, he surveyed the diverse crowd before him, his eyes never settling on anyone in particular. Still, as Geoffry and Billy watched, it appeared that each individual was left with the impression that he personally was being scrutinized, that absolutely *nothing* escaped Smith's attentive eye. Finally, the Captain cleared his throat and spoke in a firm, clear voice:

"Gentlemen, sailors, indentures, servants ~ whatever your status, you will now *all* contribute your energies to the task set for us by Captain Newport. A strong, secure fortress is our primary order of business. No one will be excused from the necessary labor. *No one!* Do you all understand?"

As Captain Smith paused briefly as though to emphasize his point, one of the more ostentatiously clothed "gentlemen" pushed to the front of the group, delicately flipping back the lace cuff at his wrist and straightening the plume on his velvet hat as he did so. "See here, my good man, surely you can't mean *everyone* is to participate in your project. Why, that is exactly the reason we brought with us our trusted and loyal servants. I shall be delighted to have my man Wiggins, here, be part of your labor force, whilst I shall personally observe to insure he does not shirk his duties." He bowed slightly, then stepped back with a self-satisfied smirk, looking around at his peers for confirmation. Nods and murmurs of approval indicated their agreement.

With cat-like agility, Captain Smith sprang to confront the aristocratic spokesman. Grasping the velvet lapels of the offender's coat in both hands, the diminutive Smith pulled the alarmed dandy down to within inches of his own face.

"Now you listen to me, you foppish popinjay," the Captain spoke through clenched teeth, "I said *everyone* would share equally in the labor. *Everyone!* Do you understand?" He shook the cowering "gentleman" roughly. *"Everyone!* Yes, your man Wiggins will join in the work ~ *and so will you!"*

These last words were uttered precisely, deliberately, each with clipped clarity, leaving absolutely *no* room for doubt regarding the Captain's intentions. Then with a look of scornful disdain, he shoved the no-longer swaggering "gentleman" back into the midst of his fellow patricians and returned to address the group.

"From here on," Smith continued in his previous calm tone, "you will be organized into working groups, each group with a specified task. I will personally oversee all activities and be available to answer questions. The fort will be constructed of logs, since timber is plentiful here. And the ships' cannon will provide the needed firepower. By the way, are there any amongst you with surveying experience?"

One hand rose hesitantly. "I done a bit o' surveyin', sir."

"Good! Anyone else?" When there was no further response, the Captain's eyes swept slowly over the crowd until they lighted on Geoffry and Billy Bascomb, standing near the edge of the group. "You two, over there! You will help us lay out the dimensions of the fort. All the rest of you will be assigned to cut down trees to clear the area that will fall within the fort's boundaries. Do I make myself perfectly understood? Now, gather your tools and follow me, and I will lead you to the designated site."

As the men set about procuring their implements, Captain Smith turned to add a final comment: "And for those of you dressed in your best finery, I would strongly suggest that you return to your campsites and put on more suitable working clothes. We will *not* be serving high tea today!"

Chapter 7

"What did you say your names were?" Captain Smith asked, as the company moved toward the site he had designated.

"Hibbard, sir. Edward Hibbard," replied the man who had indicated some knowledge of surveying.

"I'm Geoffry Payne, sir. And this is Billy Bascomb. But we're not surveyors, sir."

"You'll learn quick enough, I suspect. Now, while I put the rest of this motley crew to work chopping down trees, you three start marking out a line directly parallel to the river. Start right here, and measure straight along for exactly four hundred and twenty feet. Is that understood?"

"Yes, sir. Four hundred and twenty feet it is."

During the ensuing days, the rough outlines of James Fort gradually began to emerge. The fortress was laid out in the shape of a triangle, the prescribed four hundred and twenty feet running along the river where the water was deepest, with three-hundred-foot sides that joined at the rear. The walls were constructed of heavy logs set on end and lashed together, the lower portion dug firmly into the ground. At the corners, raised earthen bulwarks provided platforms for cannon brought from the ships. The cleared area enclosed by the walls was about an acre in size, enough space for settlers to erect crude huts or tents along with some small storage bins.

Constantly overseeing every element of the project was Captain John Smith ~ pushing, prodding, cajoling as he drove the sweating laborers and reluctant "gentlemen" to their best efforts. He seemed to be everywhere, allowing nothing to escape his watchful scrutiny. "Keep at it, men," was his constant admonition.

"Then when we're finished, you can go hunt for gold." Despite protests and complaints, the work progressed steadily.

An unfortunate series of occurrences served to demonstrate the wisdom of Smith's exhortations. As part of his effort to instill a semblance of discipline and order in the group, he had early on established a twenty-four-hour a day security watch around the area, rotating these duties through the entire company. Often in the dark of night Smith would appear personally at the designated stations to ensure that the "guards" were indeed awake and alert, not shirking their responsibilities.

Thus it was that one early morning found Pike Perliss strolling along the perimeter of the palisade, fulfilling his turn at guard duty as ordered. As might also be expected, his usual desultory manner was not improved by any sense of communal responsibility. "This's jist plain iggerant," he grumbled to himself. "Here I is, hungry an' needin' m' sleep, an' instead I gots ta walk aroun' pertectin' a bunch o' good-fer-nuthin' worthless logs what ain't goin' nowheres nohow." He shook his head in disgust, then glanced around to be sure no one was watching. Apparently unobserved, he decided he could safely sit and rest for a while.

As Perliss lingered in the nebulous realm between sleep and wakefulness, a slight movement, a shadow in the woods some distance away, caught his disoriented attention and brought him back to confused wakefulness. Focusing more clearly, he thought he detected a hazy figure moving stealthily among the trees. With no challenge, no warning whatsoever, Pike raised his musket to his shoulder, took aim, and fired.

A sharp cry from the woods, along with the echoing reverberations of the musket shot, quickly brought a number of settlers running to the scene in the dawning light.

"What's goin' on, Pike? Who's out there?"

"What happened? What ya shootin' at?"

"I thinks I seen one o' them thievin' heathen sneakin' aroun' out there, I did, prob'ly plannin' ta murder us all in'ar sleep," Pike yelled. "See, over there, in them trees?" He pointed towards the woods. "Tha's where I seen 'im. But I thinks I got th' bloody blighter! I thinks I got 'im!"

Cautiously, with weapons ready, the men approached the spot indicated by Pike. There, half hidden in the tangled underbrush, lay the crumpled figure of a young native, blood oozing from a gaping wound to his chest. His wide dark eyes drifted slowly over the threatening ring of men, reflecting astonished disbelief rather than fear. Then the brightness faded, his breath caught in a rasping gasp, and life was gone.

"*Told* ya I got the beggar, I did!" Pike exulted. "That'll learn 'im, sure anuff! Ain't *no* savage sneaks up on ol' Pike, nosiree!"

Into the gathered circle strode Captain Smith. Taking in the situation at a quick glance, he demanded, "What's going on here? Who shot this man?"

"*I* done it, Cap'n," declared Pike, ambling forward with a self satisfied swagger. "I got 'im, I did! He were tryin' ta sneak inta the fort, he was, likely plannin' nuthin' but evil fer all o' us! But Ol' Pike showed 'im what's what, he did. I showed 'im good!" He glanced around, grinning broadly, waiting for the congratulations he obviously thought were well deserved.

They were not forthcoming. "You blithering *idiot!*" bellowed Captain Smith in unabashed frustration and anger. "Do you realize what you've *done?* Look here!" he pointed to an object lying beside the now motionless body. "Do you see that?"

It was a woven basket from which had spilled ears of corn, nuts, and an assortment of berries.

Appearing almost beside himself with futile rage, Captain Smith strode over to confront the suddenly humbled Perliss. Though far smaller than the burly bully, Smith rose up on his toes until his face was scant inches from that of Perliss. "He was bringing *food*, you stupid fool!" Smith roared. "He was coming in *friendship*, bringing a gift of food, which we could certainly all use!" Thumping Perliss's chest for emphasis, he went on, "We might have been able to set up *trade* with his tribe."

"I were only doin' m' duty, Cap'n," a subdued Perliss whined. "Don't ya see? I di'n't know…."

"No, you certainly *don't* know. You don't know *anything*, you thick-headed, dimwitted, addle-pated…!" The Captain halted, as though at a loss for words to more adequately express his unqualified fury. With a final shove to Perliss's chest, he stepped over to where the body of the native lay, still muttering his profound displeasure: "He came in friendship, bringing a *gift*, and this is our response."

Smith examined the lifeless form more closely. "Look at his dress, and these painted markings," he said, pointing. "This was no ordinary native, that's for sure. This was someone of *importance.*" Shaking his head as he surveyed the gathering settlers, the Captain exclaimed, "And now there'll be the devil to pay, you can bet on that!" With a last withering look at Pike Perliss, he turned and stalked back to the fort.

Smith's observation proved to be prophetic. The young tribesman had apparently not approached the fort alone. His companions, warned by the sound of the gunshot, had quickly taken cover. From their hiding places, they had evidently witnessed the lingering death of their companion, as well as the confrontation between Captain Smith and the surly Perliss. Once the settlers returned to their fortress, the natives seemed to have made their way quietly back to their not-too-distant village to report what had occurred. Such information would have to be relayed immediately to the high chief, the werowance over all of the tribes of the area. Obviously a strong response was called for! And for the insulted natives, as among societies almost universally, the response would be a demand for *revenge!*

Back at the fort, Smith urged the settlers on to even greater effort to complete their still unfinished bastion. "Come on, men, there's no time to lose! We can't know *what* to expect, what with the death of that young Indian. And you can bet his tribe won't just forget this! So keep at it, men, keep at it! This is the only protection we have!"

As usual, Geoffry Payne and Billy Bascomb were among the laborers, working diligently to hasten completion of the palisade.

"Seems like these here logs just gets heavier ever' day, don't it?" Billy grunted as the two struggled to set one more timber upright in its proper place. "Sure wish we could find us another one o' them surveyin' jobs instead, don't you, mate?"

Geoffry laughed. "That didn't last too long, did it? So now we're just regular work-horses, like everybody else."

Once the log had been slipped into its trench and fastened securely, Geoffry stopped briefly to mop perspiration from his forehead. He glanced around, truly amazed at what Captain Smith had been able to accomplish through his regimen of strict discipline and shared labor. There were the reluctant "gentlemen," mingled with servants and craftsmen, all doing their part whether willingly or not. They still grumbled and complained, of course: "Egad! Who does that upstart commoner think he is, anyway?" or, "I say, back home in merry ol' England, he'd get his come-uppance soon enough, by Jove!" But the complaints ceased whenever the stern Captain appeared as he made his rounds.

Geoffry noted with a sense of genuine compassion the discomfort many of these "gentlemen" must be enduring, unaccustomed as they were to labor such as this. Days of wielding an axe or adz had quickly worn out their lace-fringed silk gloves. By now their hands had become severely blistered from the constant toil, yet there was no respite. Rags wrapped as protection were quickly blood-stained, leaving only the hope that perhaps calluses would eventually make the ordeal more tolerable. Geoffry was thankful that his own work-hardened, stone-bruised hands spared him from a similar fate.

The two companions returned to their seemingly endless cycle of hoisting timbers into place. But once again Geoffry halted, this time to look around for the omnipresent Captain. Smith was nowhere to be seen, apparently occupied elsewhere at the moment.

"Hey, Billy, I just thought of something," Geoffry said in a low voice. "When this James Fort is finally finished, we're going to want to fly the good old Union Jack from the ramparts, aren't we?"

"'Course we are, mate! You betcha! Ya got somethin' in mind?"

"Well, if we're going to fly a flag, we'll have to have a flag pole, won't we? And I think I know exactly where to find one."

"Ya don't say! And azzackly where might that be, mate?"

"Remember when we were scouting around the area while we were 'surveyors,' laying out the perimeter of the fort? Well, there's a place out there where I saw some young trees that looked like they'd make perfect flagpoles ~ straight as an arrow, and about the right height. I think we should go cut one down. We can surprise Captain Smith with it."

"Sounds mighty good to me, mate. Don't see the Cap'n 'round nowheres right now" ~ Billy checked the area again ~ "so it looks like we oughta be able to sneak off for a spell, alright."

Making their way to the nearby woods, Geoffry and Billy crept toward the area where he had seen the tall, straight trees. Their approach was cautious, wary, making every effort to remain as quiet as possible.

Suddenly Geoffry stopped still, signaling Billy with a gesture to do the same. Something or someone was moving noiselessly through the forest ahead of them! Both men crouched behind a pile of brush, then gradually raised their heads and focused intently on the spot Geoffry pointed out, where he had seen the movement.

It came once more: a shadow, a slight stir in the tall weeds, a flicker of change in the underbrush, all unaccompanied by any sound whatever. Geoffry and Billy glanced anxiously at each other ~ alert, tense, not moving a muscle. For some minutes they detected no further disturbances, and the two began to relax, thinking they must have been mistaken, that they had encountered nothing more sinister than a forest animal. Then, just as they were about to rise and continue with their quest, the mysterious movement recurred.

This time, however, there could be no doubt. As the two startled men watched, a figure clad only in a buckskin breech-cloth, his face and body painted in fearsome patterns, rose slowly, silently from behind a shrub some distance ahead. After scanning the surrounding area, the man gave a soundless signal, and other natives appeared at his side as if by magic. More and more gathered, and Geoffry noted with alarm that all were fully armed: bows and arrows, spears, clubs, stone tomahawks were in evidence everywhere. The group appeared to be determining its strategy.

With an insistent motion for Billy to follow, Geoffry edged back slowly, silently, step by step, remaining behind cover until both were finally at a safe distance. Turning to his wide-eyed companion, Geoffry whispered an urgent directive: "C'mon, Billy, we've got to make a run for the fort *right now!* We've got to warn Captain Smith! It looks like those warriors are planning an *attack* on James Fort!"

Chapter 8

▼

"Captain Newport! Captain Smith! Listen, everybody, *listen!* There's *Indians* out there, right over there in the woods. They've got weapons! I think they're planning to attack the fort! Hurry up, get ready! *Quick!*"

Geoffry shouted his warning as he and Billy sprinted back toward the fort. His cry of alarm brought instant action. Captain Newport dropped the chart he'd been studying and immediately sprang forward to survey the situation. Then he turned and barked out orders:

"You there, you men pile up those extra logs for a barricade at that gap near the back of the fort. That's where they'll most likely try to break through! The rest of you, go get your weapons and powder. And get back here as fast as you can!"

Captain John Smith, meanwhile, commandeered a group of settlers digging trenches: "Leave those shovels, men, and give me a hand here! These cannon need to be turned to face the rear. Toward the back there, where the walls aren't finished yet. That's our weakest point, so that's probably where they'll attack!"

For once, there was no malingering. Even the haughty "gentlemen" were caught up in the excitement of a threatened assault and appeared promptly, servants bearing their weapons and supplies of lead and powder.

"I say, where *are* those dastardly beggars?"

"Bring 'em on, by thunder! It'll be a bloody good shoot, what?"

"Right-o! Rather like hunting birds back home, don't you know!"

The rush of activity had not come a moment too soon. For now, with heart-stopping shrieks and shrill war-whoops, the attackers rose from their hiding places and burst toward the fort. It was a determined, concentrated assault, aimed as expected at that portion of the fort where palisades had not yet been completed. The swiftness and ferocity of the charge added to the confusion among the untrained, untested defenders, and many simply turned and fled.

It was at this crucial juncture that the much-maligned "gentlemen" at last demonstrated true usefulness. Some had actual military experience, others had served in local guard units back home, and all prided themselves on their ability and knowledge in handling firearms. Whether through hunting clubs or through game-management on their estates, most had become familiar with the intricacies of loading and firing muskets. That factor now proved to be a vital, life-saving advantage.

As the unwavering surge of attackers reached the vulnerable rear wall, they were met by a blazing volley from behind the log barricades. Shrieks and exultant cries died abruptly, as did mutilated natives falling among the timbers.

Astonishment and awe at the devastation caused by this unexpected and fearsome new type of weaponry brought a halt to the assault. Dazed and confused, the attackers milled around, their angry eyes sweeping the line of defenders as though in search of one particular individual. Then a second volley burst abruptly upon them from the protection of the barricades, bringing further death and terror. With agonizing cries of bewilderment, the survivors turned and fled across the clearing to the relative safety of the nearby woods.

Shouts of triumph and elation broke spontaneously from the defenders. They had won the day! Congratulatory back-slapping was accompanied by boastful assertions of English fighting prowess.

"What did I tell you, old boy? I *knew* those savages were no match for proper English firepower."

"Right-o! A bit of English pluck and discipline wins out every time, what?"

Captain Smith intervened, indicating that he was not as certain of definitive victory. "Good job, men, good job! But stay down, and keep your weapons primed. I don't think those warriors are ready to give up just yet."

"Just *let* 'em try again!" came the condescending response. "We'll give 'em more of the same, what say men?"

"Aye, that we will! Bring the blighters on!"

Laughter and more derogatory expressions from the "gentlemen" reflected their casual air of superiority. In their opinions, it seemed, Smith's concerns were baseless, nothing more than an annoying nuisance.

Geoffry and Billy were now beckoned over to where Captain Newport stood consulting with John Smith. "I'm told you two were the ones who first gave the alert. Is that right?" Captain Newport inquired.

"Well, uh, yes, sir, I believe we were, sir."

The Captain leaned forward, peering intently at Geoffry. "Haven't we met before, young man?" Then his face brightened. "Of course! You're the one who first sighted land when we got to Virginia, aren't you? That *was* you, wasn't it?"

"Yes, sir, that was me."

"And your name....your name is Payne! Do I remember correctly?"

"Yes, sir."

"Well, well, Payne! And now you're first to give a warning to the fort!" A bemused smile crossed Captain Newport's face, and he added with a laugh, "I suppose you're still waiting for your gold nugget, too, aren't you?"

Geoffry chuckled. "I guess that may have to wait a bit longer, sir. At least until the fort is completed, that is."

Now it was Captain John Smith's turn to step forward, and he looked sharply at both Geoffry and Billy Bascomb.

"What were you two doing out there in the woods, anyway? Weren't you supposed to be setting up timbers?"

Geoffry glanced at Billy, whose eyes flashed a shadow of fear. Would the stern Captain find dereliction of duty an offense even greater than the good accomplished by their warning? Before either man could respond, however, they noted a slight smile playing across Smith's face as he went on: "Well, never mind. You did a great service by sounding the alarm." He turned to Captain Newport. "I'm not sure *what* would have happened if we'd been caught completely by surprise. And I still think we'd better stay alert, prepared for a second attack."

"I believe you're right, Captain," Newport responded. "Let's go see about shoring up those barricades, and make sure we have all available powder and shot on hand." As they set out to put these preparations into effect, Captain Newport turned once more to Geoffry and Billy. "Good job, men. Carry on now."

Pride at the commendation, mingled with relief that they had not been severely reprimanded, buoyed both Geoffry and Billy as they returned to work. "Blimey! Wasn't that there *somethin'* now, mate?" Billy exclaimed in hushed tones. "Both 'o them Cap'ns, and us gettin' congradalated an' all? Who'd a' ever thunk it?"

"Yeah, Billy, you're right: 'Who'd a' ever thunk it?' But I guess now we'd better lend a hand around here, getting things ready, just in case there really *is* another attack."

All doubt regarding a second assault was erased with suddenness and fury. This time there was no warning, no paralyzing scream, no terrifying clamor. Instead, the natives had crept noiselessly, unobserved, to within mere yards of

James Fort. Now they sprang from their places of concealment in a swift, silent onslaught against the unsuspecting defenders. Firing flint or bone-tipped arrows from short bows with deadly effect, they erupted in a headlong rush through the gap in the fort's rear wall.

Determined settlers responded as speedily as possible, wielding knives, clubs, axes, whatever was at hand in a valiant attempt to repel the attackers. Others, unarmed, grappled viciously in stubborn, unyielding hand-to-hand opposition. The unprepared "gentlemen," now making belated attempts to reload their weapons, cursed helplessly as they tried to help stem the tide with feeble, scattered firepower.

Into this desperate situation broke the resolute voice of Captain John Smith, commanding: "Settlers, take cover! Cannoneers, *fire!*" At his order, bursts of deadly shot erupted from the mouths of the two ships' cannons, now aimed directly at the breach in the rear wall. Metal balls, chain, ragged pieces of shrapnel ripped through the unsuspecting cluster of natives with devastating effect, leaving only mangled carnage in their wake. Perhaps as horrifying as the path of grisly death was the cannon's belching roar, its flash of fire and smoke, the *consternation* caused by its destructive power. For a lingering instant, those warriors who had been spared seemed to freeze, wide-eyed, paralyzed with terror. Then, screaming, they rushed in a panic-stricken retreat back through the break in the wall and away from the fort, fading into the familiar woods.

Once again, cheers rose from the ranks of the defenders. But this time there was no exhibition of swaggering bravado. Rather, it was a subdued celebration, tempered by the knowledge that only extreme good fortune and superior fire-power had enabled them to survive.

And the attack had not been without cost. Among the settlers were eleven wounded, some severely ~ struck by arrows or suffering from the blows of stone-headed tomahawks and stout wooden clubs. But the deepest, most compelling loss became apparent when Captain Newport slowly stepped forward holding in his arms the lifeless form of a young boy, not more than ten or twelve years of age. The fair blonde hair was matted and blood-soaked, the result of a bludgeoning blow from some primitive yet lethal weapon.

"Robbie was my cabin-boy aboard the Susan Constant," the Captain stated in low, choked tones. "He was a fine lad, hoping to find a better life here in this New World." Captain Newport paused, struggling to gain control over what were obviously deep-felt emotions. Finally, looking down at the now still face of the small boy, he concluded quietly, "The best we can do at this point to show our respect is see that the lad gets a decent Christian burial." With that, the Captain turned and carried his diminutive burden back to his quarters.

Chapter 9

If there was any positive lesson to be learned from the attack on James Fort, it was that the unfinished fortifications needed to be *completed,* and as rapidly as humanly possible! Accordingly, the colonists set about their tasks with renewed vigor and enthusiasm in the ensuing days. Palisades were soon erected along the entire rear section where the assault had taken place, with an additional bulwark and cannon placed at the triangle where the walls met. The effect was to engender a new sense of safety and security for the settlers.

It was at this juncture that Captain Newport issued a decree: "On Sunday next, all colonists will gather for the first regular religious service to be held in our new settlement. It will be a day to give thanks for survival from attack and to celebrate Holy Communion, in conformity with the traditional rites of the Church of England."

Since no church building had yet been constructed, on the appointed day a section of ships' sail was stretched between several trees, a crude altar set up under this protective awning, and the chaplain of the "Susan Constant" conducted the prescribed liturgy. As Geoffry and Billy participated in the ritual, both were left with the feeling that somehow they were experiencing an enduring, civilizing force, a touch of home even though they were now an ocean away in a vast wilderness.

"It wasn't exactly Sunday morning in Salisbury," Geoffry observed as the two returned to their makeshift camp. "But somehow it left me with the feeling that we English are over here to stay. How about you, Billy?"

"Right ya are, mate. Made me feel kinda like this *here's* our home now, it did. Not like we's just here to get rich, an' all."

During the days that followed, Captain Newport appeared to gain enough confidence in the colony's progress to permit his return to England for fresh supplies. He ordered the crews of all three ships, still anchored in the James River, to complete preparations for sailing. Since there had been little time up to now for anything other than the work essential to establishing their settlement, the Council of Virginia decreed that the other colonists would remain behind, but would be free for the present to pursue their *own* interests. A three-month's stockpile of provisions was deemed adequate to sustain the adventurers until the Captain returned.

To avoid being forced to appear before the London Company investors empty-handed, the ships all contained small cargoes of clapboard. These rough boards had been laboriously hand-sawed by workmen assigned to that task while the other settlers had been engaged in building the stockade.

Producing clapboard was a tedious, time-consuming job. First, trench-like pits had to be dug. On each side of these trenches, pairs of sturdy posts were set in the ground, spaced about four feet apart. Two timbers were then placed across the trench at right angles, raised a few feet, and lashed firmly to the upright "legs" to create a crude platform. A log was next laid along this platform parallel to the trench, and a team of sawyers, one above and one below in the trench, proceeded to cut the logs lengthwise with their two-man saw, creating coarse boards. While such crude lumber would not provide the instant wealth anticipated by the investors, it would serve to demonstrate to the London Company the *potential* for profitable raw materials available from their new settlement.

And to further the dream that precious metals from the New World were indeed still a distinct possibility, Captain Newport also included in his lading a quantity of large stones. These had been unearthed by workmen during the process of erecting the palisades of Fort James and had immediately piqued a great deal of interest. The stones were found to be veined with a glittering material ~ believed by the eager treasure-seekers almost certainly to be gold! As excitement reigned, the stones had been carefully set aside to await an opportunity for a more careful assay. Now they would be taken to England in hopes that their great value could be verified once and for all.

Settlers gathered on the riverbank to watch the ships depart, waving and cheering the little fleet as it set sail downstream aided by the outgoing tide. A spirit of high expectancy and general optimism still prevailed. But beneath the surface, the realities surrounding their still tenuous situation, the first complexities to cloud their golden horizons, had already begun to appear. Now, with the departure of Captain Newport, their most forceful and respected leader, these nascent difficulties were about to erupt.

For some time, colonists had been complaining about the brackish drinking water, contaminated whenever incoming tides pushed salt water up the low-lying James River. With primary effort oriented toward completing the fort, the men had not taken time to dig proper wells or search for other sources of fresh water. Further, as summer heat and humidity came on, workmen found the unfamiliar climate sapping their strength and energy more and more. Additionally, the question of an adequate diet remained a problem that worsened daily as food supplies spoiled in the heat and dwindled in spite of the abundance of wild game in the forests. And finally there was the problem of rampant dysentery, "the bloody flux," brought on by lack of sanitation that made life ever more miserable.

The greatest threat of all, actually, stemmed from the *location* of their little settlement. Chosen for its defensibility against marauding Spanish men-of-war, James Fort had been built on virtual swampland. With the warming climate, bogs produced hordes of mosquitoes, often carrying dread malaria. Fevers raged, leaving settlers so weakened and debilitated they found it constantly more difficult to complete essential tasks.

Given these adverse conditions, it was small wonder that death soon began to stalk the colony. Day after day, more and more weakened settlers succumbed. Day after day, somber funeral processions set forth through the gates of the fort to the little cemetery. Steadily, ominously the number of colonists remaining healthy enough to insure success for their grand venture was diminished.

For the moment at least, Geoffry Payne and Billy Bascomb were spared, due in part to their own individual resourcefulness and cooperative efforts. They supplemented their meager rations with daily forays into the woods in search of wild berries, nuts, and edible greens. And Billy demonstrated an uncanny practical knowledge in setting snares to catch small animals or birds, utilizing techniques that never ceased to amaze his friend.

"Where on earth did you ever *learn* all those things, Billy? How do you always seem to know just exactly what to do?"

"Ah, it ain't nothin,' really, mate," came the modest reply. But the pleased look on Billy's face belied his diffidence. "It's just stuff I learned from my ol' Mum, it is. She was really somethin,' she was, always havin' to do without an' all and still tryin' to look out for us. So I guess she just natural learned some tricks to help her get along, she did, and I reckon I just natural learned 'em from her."

Fate was not as kind to many of the other adventurers, however, as men continued to fall ill, grow worse, and finally perish, including a member of the Council of Virginia itself, Captain Gosnold. With his death, plots and in-fighting amongst the rest of the Council members escalated, aggravating an already depressing situation. Work came to a practical standstill, and hope for survival of the settlement or for any of its inhabitants grew dimmer almost by the hour.

Then, as if to turn discouragement into downright desperation, a ruinous fire struck James Fort. Though no one seemed to know how it originated ~ whether from a careless campfire or perhaps from a faulty "mud and wattle" chimney ~ the effects of the fire were devastating. Structures, supplies, clothing, equipment, ammunition, all already in short supply, were destroyed. The disheartened settlers could only wonder if all of this was some sort of "sign," a manifestation of Divine disapproval or heavenly retribution, since even their newly-built little church was left in ashes. Spirits already at low ebb sank even further.

Fortunately, a saving spark of leadership emerged during this crisis, and from a most unlikely source: Captain John Smith. Out of the wrangling and quarreling of the Virginia Council, Smith emerged as the one person able to take control, to instill enough discipline and order to prevent total disintegration of the colony. And despite continued resentment and bickering at his "usurpation of power," the desperate straits of the settlers forced them, however reluctantly, to obey his edicts. It was to be an uneasy alliance, as he soon realized.

Calling together all those still able-bodied enough to assemble, Captain Smith issued his orders:

"Our first concern from here on will be to preserve the limited food supplies we still have on hand. Therefore, I am placing all remaining stores directly under my own personal supervision, to be rationed equally to all as needed. The storehouse will be rebuilt, and a guard will be posted to ensure that supplies are distributed only in accordance with this regulation."

Ignoring the scattered mutterings of protest, Smith continued: "Secondly, we must all strive to improve our temporary shelters while this weather holds. Spaces will be allotted within the walls of the fort, and I urge everyone to begin building some type of suitable structure to provide protection from the elements."

Protests grew louder, punctuated by expressions of strong disagreement:

"What's wrong with where we're living *now*?"

"Yeah! Why do you have to try to *change* everything?"

"Right! We won't be here long anyway, so why waste our efforts building shelters when we could be looking for *gold* instead?"

Smith's response was unequivocal: *"Silence!* This is *not* Parliament, and these rules are *not* up for debate. They apply to *all*, and you <u>will</u> obey them! *Is that clear?"*

From one of the "gentlemen" came a curt rejoinder: "Look here, my good man, we know you mean well and all, but we are subjects of the *Crown*, not of you. How do you propose to *enforce* such arbitrary rules? What if we decide *not* to obey?"

As Geoffry, standing not far away, observed Captain Smith's reaction to this defiant query, he feared for a moment that the former soldier was on the verge of challenging the arrogant spokesman to a duel. However, after a long pause during which Smith's eyes appeared to literally bore into his adversary, the Captain drew a deep breath: "There will be one standard that applies to *all*, as I said, and one standard only. It is this: *He who does not work, shall not eat!* Do you all *understand?*"

The vehemence with which the dictum was pronounced left absolutely no room for question or argument. Its finality was emphasized both by its brevity and by its clarity. All appeared to realize that from now on *this* concept would be the *law!*

With dissent effectively stifled as a result of his forceful rejoinder, Smith concluded: "Now, while you all go about your tasks, I shall select a few of our number to accompany me in exploring the surrounding countryside. We *must* try to make friendly contact with the natives, to establish trade with them if possible to obtain food. Our current supplies cannot last long, as you well know. They must be supplemented by food from the neighboring tribes, as well as from gardens that I urge you to begin planting as soon as your other tasks are completed.

"If I am successful in my endeavors with the Indians, there is hope that our present hardships can and will be alleviated. If not..." He paused for a long moment, then finished in a brusque tone, "All right, it's time for everyone to *get back to work!*"

Chapter 10

"Hey, mate look over there. Cap'n Smith's surely talkin' mighty serious 'bout somethin' with them two gentlemens, ain't he now?"

"Yeah, you're right, Billy. Wonder what's going on?"

"Ya don't s'pose he's ax'in' 'em to join up with that esplorin' party he was talkin' about, now do ya? Not *them* worthless no-goods!"

"No, I don't think he's really too fond of their sort. Much too sophisticated for their own good, and way too lazy!"

"Sure wish *we* was goin' with him, though, don't you, mate, 'stead o' havin' to stay here cuttin' down more trees, an' all? Blimey! Looks like we'll be cuttin' down trees 'til we dies, it does!"

"Careful, Billy! The Captain's coming this way. Give me a hand with this timber, will you?"

As they went on with their work, a firm voice broke in, halting their efforts: "You two ~ Payne, Bascomb! I'd like a word with you."

The friends stood waiting as the Captain approached. But there was no way whatever that they could have anticipated what he had in mind as he greeted them: "You heard what I said a while ago about forming a party to explore the area beyond the fort, didn't you?"

"Yes sir, Captain, we sure did." The response came almost in unison.

"Well, I'd like you two to be part of my group. Will that be a problem for either of you?"

"No, *sir*, not at all! Not a bit! We'd be real *happy* to join you, sir! Wouldn't we, Billy?"

"That we would, sir, that we surely would, an' no mistake! Yes *sir!*"

"Then it's settled. I'll get the rest of my group together as soon as possible and we'll get started first thing tomorrow morning. Is that understood?"

"Yes, sir! Tomorrow morning it is, sir."

Both men snapped Captain Smith their best salutes before returning to their shelter, their spirits soaring with anticipation and excitement.

"Can ya *believe* it, mate? *Us,* goin' esplorin' with the Cap'n, an' all?"

"Yeah, who'd have ever guessed we'd be so lucky! Wow! How about that, Billy?"

Both woke very early the next morning, eager and anxious to get started. They gathered their gear and what few supplies they could collect, then headed for the designated rendezvous spot. Captain Smith was already there, waiting. As it turned out, only two other men had been selected for the Captain's special project ~ both known to have previous military experience. Now they came hurrying up, muskets in hand.

Smith immediately got down to business. "Men, our mission will be to explore the country to the north of James Fort. Now we know that Captain Newport also took a group in that direction once before. They went up the James River, looking for the fabled passage to India, but they ran into waterfalls and couldn't get through.

"But he told me about *another* river, one that branches *off* the James, called the Chickahominy. And that one just *may* be the waterway we've been looking for. We'll see."

Then, as though to indicate his own personal skepticism regarding the actual *existence* of such a passageway, Smith added, "Anyway, even if we *don't* find this 'gateway to the Orient,' at least we may be able to contact some Indian tribes in the area willing to share a few supplies with us. You all know how desperately we need food right now!"

Captain Smith had procured a small boat, and into this the exploring party loaded their goods. Once the men had boarded and arranged themselves according to Smith's directions, the little party shoved off, heading up the James River with Geoffry and Billy manning the oars as best they could against the slow-moving current.

Nothing untoward occurred to impede their leisurely progress, but all were awed by the natural beauty of their sylvan surroundings. Approximately ten miles upriver they came to a tributary emptying into the James ~ a smaller stream that branched off to the right. "That *should* be the Chickahominy," Captain Smith surmised. "Turn in here, and let's see where it goes."

As they proceeded up the new watercourse, it soon became evident that this was *no* grand passage to the Far East. The river narrowed quickly, and before long the branches of trees growing on opposite banks linked overhead to form a luxuriant canopy.

Captain Smith ordered a halt. "We'll go ashore here and proceed on foot. It's pretty obvious we're not going to reach China this way."

After guiding their little boat to the riverbank, Geoffry stepped out and secured the craft to a large oak. The others assembled under its spreading branches, bringing with them their small stores of supplies and equipment.

As the group bustled about, assessing the situation before determining their next move, Geoffry stopped abruptly, motionless, fully alert. His eyes focused intently on a spot just beyond the little clearing, certain he had detected some type of movement, a brief stir among the trees. Signaling the others, he maintained a close watch on the area. It seemed eerie, almost like a reenactment of what he and Billy had experienced in the woods behind James Fort!

Slowly, cautiously a figure emerged from behind a giant cypress where he had apparently been observing the strangers. Armed with nothing but a stout staff, clad only in a buckskin loincloth, the native appeared to pose no immediate threat. As though to emphasize his amicable intentions, he raised his left hand slowly, palm forward in a sign of peace, and moved toward the group.

The men waited for Captain Smith to provide direction. Still, the two with muskets kept their weapons trained on the visitor, ready for any sign of treachery. "Easy, men," the Captain cautioned. "Let's see what he wants. But stay alert, stay ready. We can't be sure what he's up to."

Smith stepped into the open, raising his hand in a return salute. The Indian continued his approach, watchful yet indicating no evidence of fright. When only a few feet separated the two men, he halted.

"Wawoka. Pamunkey," the native stated in a clear voice, pointing to himself.

"Captain John Smith. English," came the reply. Then Smith recalled a name, one given him by Captain Newport. It was the name of the head chief, or werowance, over *all* the tribes of the region, someone who had treated Newport with respect and graciousness during the Captain's earlier explorations. Smith pointed toward the north and inquired, "Powhatan?"

The eyes of the Indian widened momentarily in surprise, then a smile gradually creased the bronzed face. "Ah, Powhatan!" He nodded, turning toward the north as he spread his arms wide. "Powhatan!" he repeated, seeming to indicate that the great chief's power extended *everywhere*.

Smith, too, smiled in response. Pointing first to the Indian, then to himself, then to the rest of his party, he asked slowly, "You take us Powhatan?"

The native appeared perplexed by the request. Shaking his head, he looked questioningly at Captain Smith. The Captain repeated his query, this time with even more elaborate gestures: "You take us to Powhatan?"

The dark eyes lighted. With a smile of comprehension breaking across his face, Wawoka pointed to his chest and stated: "Take us Powhatan!" Laughter and smiles broke the tension, and the native moved closer to join the little party. He patted each explorer on the back in turn, repeating, "Take us Powhatan!" It was indeed an encounter in marked contrast to what the men generally experienced at James Fort. There, Indians were viewed primarily as "vicious savages." Here, one on one, a truly human connection was taking place, seeming to provide a basis for genuine long-term friendship and understanding.

Since it was by now late in the day, Captain Smith told the group, "We'll stay here tonight and start out right after sunrise. It looks like maybe this chap really *can* lead us to Powhatan." Camp was set up, a small fire built to warm their meager rations, and Wawoka was invited by gestures to join them in sharing their evening meal.

With the first rays of a bright morning sun breaking through their leafy awning, Smith hustled the men into action, at the same time laying out the course upon which he had settled: "We can't take the boat any farther, that's clear, but we have to keep it safe for our return trip. Payne, Bascomb ~ I'm leaving you two here to guard the boat, while the rest of us go ahead with Wawoka to meet Powhatan. We'll see if maybe we can obtain supplies from his tribe, and if we can we'll try to bring them back this far. Then we can all make our way back down river to James Fort. Does everyone understand?"

"Yes, sir!" came the unanimous response. Geoffry felt a sharp pang of disappointment at not being allowed to accompany the Captain, to help find Powhatan's village and perhaps meet the powerful chief. Yet he knew that Smith's plan was sound, and he and Billy reluctantly gathered their gear and set their things in order at the campsite.

"We should be back in a few days, a week at most," Smith assured them. With that, the three Englishmen followed Wawoka as he led them single file down a dim pathway. Soon the little group was swallowed up by the dense forest.

"Now ain't this somethin' else again, mate?" Billy exploded as soon as the party was out of sight. "Here we was, ready to be grand esplorers of the whole bloomin' country, we was, and maybe even find a way to Chinee an' all, and look what happens! We gets stuck guardin' a bloody *boat*! I can't believe it, I can't! Nosiree!" He shook his head in disgust.

"Yeah, I don't like it much either, Billy. I was really hoping to go along and see if I could learn something about these Indian tribes. And that Wawoka seemed like a right nice chap, didn't he? But here we are."

Billy leaned closer. "D'ya s'pose we could just kinda take that boat and do some esplorin' on our *own*, like, mate? Who knows *when* Cap'n Smith'll get back, or if he ever *will?*"

Geoffry chuckled. "No, I think we'd better stay right here, Billy, like we were told. Let's at least give them a chance."

The friends settled into a daily camp routine, much of it comprised of monotonous, uninterrupted waiting. To help pass the time, Billy set up his snares for game, and both men spent hours trying to spear fish with sharpened sticks in the clear waters of the Chickahominy, though with only limited success. Still, with the wild fruit they found as they foraged through the woods and with the yield from the snares, they managed to keep themselves reasonably well fed.

A week passed, and still they waited, expecting the return of the exploring party at any moment. More days went by, and finally a second week. By now the waiting was wearing heavily on both men, intensified by concern for the safety of their companions.

"What do ya s'pose could o' *happened?*" Billy asked for perhaps the hundredth time. But neither really wanted to voice his deepest fears after having witnessed only too recently the ferocity with which the native warriors fought when provoked. "Do ya think they could o' got *lost?* Or did they maybe get *attackted* or somethin'?"

"I just don't know, Billy." Geoffry was too worried himself to be reassuring. "But we both know that if there's *any* way at all to get back, Captain Smith will find it. You can bet on that!"

As the third week of tense, worrisome waiting progressed, both Geoffry and Billy began to seriously consider returning to James Fort with the little boat in an effort to procure help. They reasoned that if the men had indeed become lost or if harm had come to them, the Council should be notified. Perhaps a rescue party could be organized to search for them.

While the two anxiously debated alternatives, they assembled their belongings, ready to move out the moment they could settle on a course of action. A sudden "Halloo" from the woods broke the uncertainty. Alarmed, both men dashed for cover behind the trunk of the oak under whose protective arbor they had been waiting. They peered out apprehensively, and were both surprised and relieved to see the familiar figure of Wawoka approaching their camp.

With a joyous shout that in turn startled the Indian, the two men rushed out to greet him. But something had changed. Though Wawoka had been very open and amiable during their first meeting, Geoffry now noted a sense of reserve, a reticence that was in marked contrast to his behavior when he had initially agreed to serve as Captain Smith's guide.

Wawoka raised his hand in greeting, but said nothing. Instead, he handed Geoffry a piece of birchbark. Perplexed, Geoffry carefully examined the bark to determine if it had any significance. As he turned it over, he saw a cryptic message scratched in crude letters: "Attacked. Held prisoner. Notify fort." It was signed simply, "J. Smith."

Chapter 11

"Hey mate, will ya look at that? Where d'ya 'spose everybody *went* to?"

Geoffry was asking himself the same question as their boat approached James Fort. The two could detect absolutely no activity, no movement, no sign of any life at all.

"D'ya think the fort might'a got *attackted* again? Or did everyone just up and *die* while we was gone?"

Geoffry could offer no explanation. "I can't *imagine* what's going on, Billy. There's no guard on duty, nobody's clearing trees, nothing. It's like the place has been *abandoned.*"

They rowed their little craft to the make-shift landing dock in front of James Fort, tied it to a piling, and headed for the entrance gate. Still there was no challenge, no greeting, no reaction of any sort from anyone.

It wasn't until they got inside the fort that they were able to ascertain what was taking place. With the departure of Captain Smith, it became apparent, every vestige of discipline, all sense of responsibility had *also* vanished. Craftsmen and indentures alike were lounging lazily about the fort in scattered groups, some playing cards, others idly chatting or otherwise passing the time. Gathered at some distance from their fellow settlers was a small circle of "gentlemen" engaged in lively conversation amongst themselves as they sipped their drinks. No one showed the slightest inclination for carrying on assigned tasks ~ either improving their own habitats or working on the fort itself.

Everywhere, too, was evidence that illness and death had in no way abated during the absence of the explorers. Men thrashed about on mats or blankets, moaning, shivering with fever, calling for water or assistance, but being mostly ignored. Others had sunk so low, were so weak, that they appeared only to be awaiting the end ~ and a final solution to their suffering and misery.

As he looked around, aghast at what he saw about him, Geoffry noted one additional factor: the door to the supply storehouse stood wide open, with neither guard nor remaining supplies to be seen anywhere. The place had been stripped clean! Apparently the attitude "every man for himself" had become the all-pervasive criterion for any actions involving the colonists. What tomorrow would bring seemed beyond consideration or concern.

Geoffry's primary duty, he realized, was to notify the Council of Virginia of the capture of Captain John Smith. Accordingly, he and Billy sought out Captain John Ratcliffe, who had emerged some time earlier as the new Council President following a further round of plots, counter-plots, and intrigue.

They located the former commander of the "Discovery" among the circle of "gentlemen" enjoying both their leisure and their libations. Approaching the gathering, Geoffry and Billy stood at a respectful distance, waiting to be acknowledged by some individual from the group. At last someone spoke up: "Yes, yes, what is it, my good man? Don't tell us you've come to beg for more rations!"

"No, not at all, sir," Geoffry replied, stepping forward. "We were members of Captain Smith's exploring party. He's been *captured!* He sent back this message." Geoffry handed over the piece of birchbark.

His words caused an immediate stir:

"What, captured, you say?"

"Finally got what he deserved, what?"

"Let's have a look at that message," came from Captain Ratcliffe. "How the devil could he...."

"I say, serves the blighter right, it does!"

"Right! Might save us the trouble o' hangin' the beastly scoundrel."

Geoffry broke into the exchange to express his anxious concerns: "Shouldn't we be organizing a rescue party, or some kind of fighting force? We can't just ignore....."

Abruptly, he was cut off by one of the "gentlemen": "Look here, old chap, you've done your duty and delivered your message. Now run along and leave this matter to your superiors. *We'll* attend to it in our own way, in our own time." Turning away, the speaker made it abundantly clear that from here on it would be absolutely none of Geoffry's concern.

It was too much for Geoffry. Though usually able to exercise reasonable restraint over his hereditary temper, he recognized at once that a grave injustice was about to be done, based purely on personal antagonisms. It was a consummate violation of his fierce sense of fair play and honor, and as a result his temper flared. Stepping boldly into the circle of detractors, he gave full vent to his mounting fury.

"Now you listen to me! Don't any of you *understand?* Captain Smith was risking his *life* for this settlement. He and two of our men have been *captured!* You can't just leave them to *die!* You just *can't!* What kind of cowards are you, anyway? They need our help, and they need it *now!*"

The flashing dark eyes, the forcefulness of Geoffry's words, stunned his listeners temporarily. But not for long.

"I say, you're a right rude bloke, aren't you now, going on like that to the likes of us!"

"Right-o! Just who do you think you are, anyway? After all, common folk like you should know their *place* and show proper respect to their betters."

Nodding heads and mutterings of agreement let Geoffry know beyond question that his tirade was *not* going to bring about the hoped-for action. Still, his outrage refused to allow him to retreat in the face of such blatant, willful apathy.

"So you're just going to sit there on your fat duffs and let three good men *die*, are you, you bunch of arrogant, superfluous scum? Well, I can tell you this: Captain Smith is worth more all by *himself* than the whole lot of you pretentious big-wigs put together!"

He continued to stand his ground, defiance and rage rooting him to the spot, until finally Captain Ratcliffe grasped his arm and led him firmly back to where Billy waited. "We appreciate your bringing us the message, young man. But I'm afraid these good gentlemen do *not* appreciate either your attitude or your candor! I think it best, now, that you both go back to your quarters and await the decision of the Council. *They're* the ones charged with conducting the affairs of this colony, after all! *They're* the ones who will ultimately decide the fate of Captain Smith. And any further outbursts on *your* part will likely end with your confinement to our guardhouse. Is that *understood?*"

Geoffry jerked his arm free, still seething with indignation. "Oh, they'll come to a decision alright, you can bet on that! They'll decide to keep on doing exactly what they're doing right now ~ which is absolutely *nothing!*" He faced the Captain directly: "But I'm especially disappointed in *you*, Captain Ratcliffe, sir. You're a good leader! Your men thought *highly* of you! And now you're siding with these phony imbeciles!" With a final withering look, Geoffry turned his back on the group, adding brusquely, "Come on, Billy, let's get out of here before any of that sickening snobbery rubs off on *us!*"

As the two headed back toward the site they had chosen for construction of their new shelter, Billy looked up at his friend, unabashed admiration sparkling in his eyes, an irrepressible grin spread broadly across his face. "Now *that* was somethin' *else*, it was, mate! That was truly somethin' else! Ya finally give them smart-alecky dandies what's what, ya did, an' no mistake! Me oh my! I reckon their ears is *still* a'flamin,' they is! Yesiree, that was *somethin'*, aw'right!"

"What a pack of parasites!" Geoffry's resentfulness had not subsided. "You can bet your life they're just going to sit there and not do *one single thing* to try to rescue either Captain Smith or our other two men. I just don't know what more to *do!* I feel so *helpless!*"

"Aw, I'm bettin' the Cap'n's gonna be alright, he is, mate. He'll find a way to get outa' trouble, just like he done when he was captured by them Turks, an' all. You just wait an' see!"

"I sure hope you're right about that, Billy. But I still don't know what *we* should be doing. Do you think we ought to go back there *ourselves* and see if we can find them and get them free somehow?"

"I was thinkin' on that myself, I was. But ya know, mate, we'd prob'ly just get *ourselves* lost out there in them woods, too, and then what? Wouldn't be no help thataway, now would we?"

"I know, Billy, I know! But it's so hard not to at least *try*. Seems like we're no better than those officious sniveling milksops this way."

"Aw, c'mon now, mate, ya shouldn't be so tough on yourself. We give our report, like the Cap'n axed, we did, so now let's first wait an' see if'n that no-'count Council might actual *do* somethin'. If'n they *don't* do nothin,' like ya says, well, after that maybe we can figger out what *we* oughta be doin.' Alright?"

With that, the pair returned to the structure they had begun working on before Captain Smith selected them to be part of his exploring expedition. They straightened some of the clutter, put their few belongings back in place. Next they decided they might as well continue with their building efforts, since there really was little else they could do. Maybe if we keep busy enough, Geoffry told himself unhappily, there won't be time to *worry* about what might be happening to Captain Smith and those other two.

The result was that their shelter actually began to take rather rapid shape. The two had been living previously in a rough lean-to erected under the brushy trees and tall cedars near the edge of the clearing. But both had been anxious for something better ~ something more permanent that would provide protection from the weather. When Captain Smith began to allocate building spaces within the confines of James Fort itself, Geoffry and Billy had been among the first to apply and were assigned a small area near the rear of the fort. Before leaving with the Captain, they had managed to lay out the general outlines of their new home and had begun to cut and gather timbers and other materials necessary for construction.

Now they went about their work with renewed enthusiasm. They had decided to utilize the traditional style of architecture and design common back in England at the time, called "mud and wattle." First they fashioned two A-shaped frameworks out of heavy timbers, hand-hewn and roughly squared. After raising these end-sections into upright position, they lashed a stout roof-beam along the top to hold the two in place. Next, two additional beams were fastened along the sides, parallel with the ground, to which would be attached a number of slats to form walls. Between the slats they planned to weave flexible twigs or branches called "wattles" and then plaster over the entire latticework with mud and allow it to dry. After that, all their little dwelling would require would be a roof ~ formed by fastening light poles from the roof-beam to the side-beams and again interlacing this framework with boughs and branches to hold the customary thatch. It would be a structure not much different from those that could be found dotting the English countryside back home.

For two days, they concentrated diligently on their building efforts, hoping in the process to escape the nagging concerns regarding their missing companions. But these hopes proved to be futile.

"I wonder if that good-for-nothing Council has decided to do anything yet about sending out a rescue party. Or are they still just sitting there, talking?"

"Ain't heard nothin' so far, mate, and small surprise it is, I tell ya!"

"You know, Billy, I think it's time *you and I* go back upriver, back to our old camp. We could try to follow that trail where Wawoka led the group into the woods. Who knows, we just might be able to find out where they went."

Their discussion was interrupted by an unexpected commotion near the entrance gate to James Fort. Excited colonists were running toward the area, gathering around someone or something apparently of great interest.

"What do ya s'pose is goin' *on* over there, mate?"

"I haven't got the faintest idea! Let's go find out!"

The two men rushed to the spot and wiggled through the milling throng. As they reached the center of activity, they stopped short ~ totally amazed, in utter disbelief! There, standing calmly in the midst of the gaping gathering with an Indian companion at his side, was Captain John Smith!

Chapter 12

"Captain Smith, sir! Wawoka! It's so good to *see* you both again!" Geoffry rushed forward and gripped the Captain's hand in a firm handshake, then clapped Wawoka on the back in friendly greeting. Billy, too, welcomed them warmly, his face a broad grin.

"Payne! Bascomb! So you made it back, did you? And you got my message?"

"That we did, sir. We delivered it to the Council here at James Fort, just like you asked."

"And what was their response?"

Geoffry looked at the ground, embarrassed. "Well, sir, I guess they haven't got around to doing much of *anything* yet." He looked uneasily at Billy, who seemed equally chagrined.

"We was just about to come lookin' for ya ourselves, we was, sir," Billy chimed in.

A momentary flash of anger lit the Captain's eyes at news of the Council's inaction, but it passed quickly. "Well, never mind, men. You both did your duty, and I thank you for that. Like that fellow back home, Shakespeare, puts it, 'All's well that ends well!'"

"Right you are, sir. But how did you manage to get *back* here? Your message said you'd been captured. How did you escape? And where are the other two men who were with us?" Geoffry's rapid-fire queries seemed to reflect the curiosity of all who had gathered around.

Captain Smith turned aside the questions with a wave of his hand, but a shadow darkened his face briefly. "All in good time, Payne, all in good time. It was an adventure I can still hardly believe myself, to tell the truth. But I'll get to that later. Right now I want to show everyone what we brought back. I'm sure it's something you'll all welcome and appreciate."

With that, Smith reached for the large buckskin bag he had dropped upon entering the fort. Wawoka held a similar bag. Untying the thongs at the top, Smith poured the contents out on the ground. The golden cascade brought first gasps of surprise, then cheers of joy from the assembled settlers as a pile of Indian corn grew before them. Wawoka added his trove to the pile, and the shouts of approval grew even louder.

The boisterous proceedings finally appeared to arouse the curiosity of the blasé "gentlemen," who had thus far viewed the gathering at the gate with practiced indifference. Now they sauntered over, led by the patronizing aristocrat who had earlier so arbitrarily dismissed Geoffry and Billy when they attempted to present their report. Elbowing through the gathering with haughty, disdainful glances both left and right, he stopped abruptly at sight of John Smith. His face flushed, and his eyes reflected disappointed surprise, as well as intense displeasure and dislike.

"So, Smith. You made it back after all, did you? It's a good job we didn't waste time and effort going searching for you as your man so rudely demanded, isn't it now?"

"My only regret, Archer," replied the Captain, "is that your abominable *lack* of effort kept you from getting lost somewhere out there in the woods *yourself. Permanently!*"

Gabriel Archer sniffed contemptuously. "Same old Smith, I see. Never one to show proper deference to those in authority, are you?"

"*Authority*, Archer? *You?* Why, you're nothing but a no-good, cheating, swindling barrister, and you know it! Authority? Ha!"

"Have a care, Smith! You may not be aware that I was elected to serve on the Council of Virginia whilst you wasted your time traipsing off through the forests. And exactly what did you accomplish, pray tell? Did you locate that passageway to India you were assigned to find? Did you come upon any of the survivors of the 'Lost Colony'? Or did you merely spend your time squandering more of the Company's resources?"

Smith took a deep breath, gaining time to compose himself. Disclosure of Gabriel Archer's appointment to the ruling Council seemed to come as a keen disappointment, since it was common knowledge in the settlement that he and Smith were bitter enemies.

"No, we didn't find any passageway, Archer, if indeed there is such a thing. Nor did we find any survivors of the 'Lost Colony.' What we *did* bring back, however, may be of far greater immediate value." He indicated the pile of Indian corn. "From the looks of things around here, it seems that proper food must be a prime priority by now."

Archer gave the corn a contemptuous glance. *"This?* This is all you have to show for your efforts? And what good is it anyway, may I ask? Surely you don't expect civilized Englishmen to eat the victuals of common aborigines, do you now?"

Captain Smith could barely contain his disgust. "No, Archer, personally I hope you don't touch one *kernel* of this corn! I hope you just starve to death instead, and the sooner the better!" He turned to Wawoka. "Come on, friend. Let's get out of here."

But Gabriel Archer wasn't through. "Now just a moment, Smith. Before you turn tail and run, I'd like to know where the rest of your so-called 'exploring party' is. You left here with five men. You and two others have returned, along with this primitive you've brought into the fort, likely to spy us out for his fellow savages. Now I demand to know: Where are the other two men?"

John Smith turned slowly, a look of deep pain and anguish on his face. "They were killed," he said softly. "We were attacked in the woods by a war party. They killed both my men, and then they took me captive." Shifting his gaze to Geoffry and Billy, he concluded, "I'm truly sorry. They were good men."

The news had a decided impact upon Gabriel Archer. "What's *this*, Smith? You took two of our men on a fool's errand and you got them *killed* by savages? Is that what I'm hearing?" When the Captain refused to respond, Archer went on: "Why, of all the rank *incompetence!* You, who style yourself a 'Captain' and boast of your grand military exploits? Well, well! The Council shall take note of this, you may be certain! Yes, indeed! Rest assured that this is not the end of the matter!"

With that Archer strode off, his mincing minions trailing behind. To Geoffry, the lawyer's feigned dismay at the loss of the two explorers appeared as nothing more than a transparent sham. Archer's sly smirk had betrayed his *true* agenda: he hoped to find some pretext, no matter how contrived or trivial, to denigrate and humble Captain John Smith.

"Do you think he plans to make trouble for you, Captain?" Geoffry asked, concerned, as they watched the "gentlemen" depart.

"Oh, I'm sure he'll try if he can figure out a way. But remember, I've managed to survive so far, haven't I, in spite of all his efforts? So we'll just have to wait and see what he's up to." Smith paused, glancing out at the James River as it flowed placidly toward the sea. "By the way, Captain Newport hasn't returned yet with those fresh supplies, has he? Wasn't he due some weeks ago?"

"We've had no word, sir. From the way things look here at the fort, though, he can't get back any too soon, that's for sure."

The settlers gradually drifted back to their day's activities, and Geoffry and Billy Bascomb returned to their interrupted building activities. It wasn't long, however, before Captain Smith approached, a look of anxious concern on his face. "I say, Payne, Bascomb, has either of you seen Wawoka? He seems to have wandered off somewhere."

"No, sir, I haven't seem him. How about you, Billy?"

"Ain't seen nary a sign of 'im, nowheres, Cap'n."

"I'll keep looking. He can't have gone far, I'm sure. It's just that he doesn't understand much of the language and.... you know!"

"We'll give you a hand, sir. Billy, why don't you check over there by the storehouse, and I'll take a look outside the gate."

Geoffry spent some time searching the area around the fort, finding nothing. As he started back to see if the other two had been more successful, he was stopped short, alerted by a low, angry voice that appeared to be coming from a wooded area nearby. Standing absolutely still, Geoffry waited, eyes focused intently, every sense attuned in an effort to identify the unexplained sound. It came again: the same low heated tones, the same muffled, snarling utterances. The voice struck him as vaguely familiar, yet he was unable to determine either who was speaking or what was being said.

Curious and wary, Geoffry edged closer. Now he could detect movement, a human shape. Could it be a party of natives, preparing for another attack on the fort? He was determined to find out.

Cautiously he continued his advance. And then the angry voice sounded again: "Still won't talk, eh? Well, I gots all day, I has. An' I says yer gonna tell me what yer doin' here, snoopin' 'roun' our fort an' all. You'll be plenty sorry if'n ya don't, ya will! Yer spyin' fer them bloodthirsty thievin' friends o' yers, ain't ya? *Ain't* ya?" There was no response. "Aha, mebbe ya jist needs a little more *cuttin'* ta convince ya ta talk, does ya now? Well, how 'bout *this?*"

At once, Geoffry knew! With no further need for quiet, he crashed through the barrier of brush and confronted his old adversary, Pike Perliss.

Tied securely to a cedar tree was the Indian guide, Wawoka, blood dripping from cuts that covered his entire upper body. His chest, his arms were crisscrossed with dozens of bleeding wounds, but still he did not utter a sound. In his eyes there was a shadow of bewilderment, but far more obvious was the glare of unrestrained hate.

Geoffry's sudden assault caught Perliss off guard. Geoffry smashed into the bully with all the force he could muster, carrying both men to the ground. Despite the ferocity of the attack, however, Perliss managed to retain possession of his knife.

"*You* again, eh, Payne?" he snarled. "Allus you, ain't it, meddlin' in where it ain't none o' yer bizness! Well, how 'bout I gives ya *this?*" He slashed furiously at his attacker.

Geoffry felt a sharp stab of pain and saw blood run from a deep gash on his forearm. The sight only heightened his rage. Circling the menacing Pike Perliss, he feigned another charge, then jumped aside just in time to avoid Pike's lunge and knife thrust. Now, like an enraged cat, he sprang, catching the flailing Perliss from behind in a bear-hug that pinned both arms tightly to his sides.

Once more Geoffry relied on the strength he had gained from long hours of stone-working. Slowly he increased a relentless pressure, ignoring the throbbing pain from the wound to his arm, while the cursing, screaming Perliss cried out in helpless rage. But it wasn't until Geoffry actually felt some of Pike's ribs give way that he finally hurled the bully to the ground and stepped back.

Writhing in agony, Perliss could only gasp out his epithets through moans of pain: "Ya blasted bloody fool, whadidya hafta go an' do *that* fer, anyways? Now you's likely *kilt* me, ya has! Innerferin' bastard!"

Ignoring Pike's invective, Geoffry scooped up the fallen knife and stepped over to Wawoka. "I'm so sorry, friend," was all he could manage by way of apology as he cut the bonds holding the Indian. "I'm so sorry!" With a beckoning gesture, he added, "Come on back to the fort with me, so we can look after those wounds."

But Wawoka only shook his head, seeming uncertain whether he could trust even this white rescuer. Slowly he raised his left hand, palm forward, then turned and disappeared silently into the forest.

Geoffry looked down at the groaning, still-prone Pike. "You just don't ever *learn*, do you, Perliss? You know very well this isn't going to be the end of all this, not by any means. We'll see what Captain Smith has to say when I report your latest stupidity." Leaving the cringing bully where he lay, Geoffry headed back toward the fort.

Before he could reach the gate, however, he saw Billy rushing toward him, agitated with excitement. "*C'mon*, mate, hurry up! We got to *do* somethin', an' right *now,* we do! Them idiot Council members just came and arrested Cap'n Smith, they did! I think they's plannin' to lock 'im up in the JAIL!"

Chapter 13

As he and Billy raced back through the gates of James Fort, Geoffry saw at once that Billy's assessment had been correct. There stood Captain John Smith, an armed guard on either side, while the members of the Council of Virginia huddled behind their spokesman, Gabriel Archer. The lawyer was reading with obvious relish a proclamation drawn up by the Council, aimed at the defiant Captain: "….and furthermore, for bringing about the untimely deaths of two of His Majesty's loyal subjects, it is hereby decreed that you are sentenced to be incarcerated in the James Fort guardhouse until further notice."

Archer finished his reading with a flourish and a mock bow to the prisoner, a look of triumph in his eyes, unable to hide his personal self-satisfaction. Smith's only response was a wry smile. Then he turned smartly on his heel and marched away between the two guards.

"Well now, did ya ever see the likes o' *that?* Did ya, now?" Billy burst out. "We has to *do* somethin' about this, mate, an' no mistake!"

"You're absolutely right, Billy. This is a frame-up, pure and simple. Let's see if we can find some way to get in and talk to Captain Smith, see if *he* has any ideas. And I've got to tell him about Wawoka, too!"

The two followed at a distance behind the departing procession until it reached the make-shift guardhouse with its single prison cell, constructed at an earlier time to provide "discipline" for the unruly. They watched as the guards unlocked the heavy guardhouse door, took their prisoner inside, then escorted him to the small cell. The guards displayed none of the malice that had been so obvious in the actions of Archer. Rather, they treated the Captain with deference and respect.

"Hey mate, I *knows* one o' them there guards, I do," Billy announced in an excited whisper. "We shipped out together once on the same tradin' ship, we did! Maybe he'll let us get inside to talk to the Cap'n."

As it turned out, the guard had no compunctions whatever about granting his old shipmate a favor. But he added a note of caution: "Just make sure ya don't let none o' them Council dandies see ya now, ya hear? I don't wanna be joinin' the Cap'n in that there cell, nosiree."

Captain Smith seemed genuinely delighted when he saw his former exploring companions approaching. "Payne, Bascomb, it's truly good to see you two! But how did you men manage to get in here?"

Following Billy's explanation, Smith gave voice to his deepest concern: "Were either of you able to find Wawoka? I'm really worried about what might have happened to him, since he doesn't know much of our language or anything."

Now it was Geoffry's turn, and he related his experience with Pike Perliss. The Captain's face darkened as Geoffry reviewed the events, deep anger flashing in his eyes. "That coward Perliss! As if he hadn't caused enough trouble already! I'm just happy you were able to help Wawoka get away."

The statement provided Geoffry an opportunity to voice the question *he* had been curious about: "Captain Smith, sir, we've all been wondering just how *you* got away when you were captured by those Indians. Would this be a good time to tell us?" He glanced around, then added with a light laugh, "Doesn't look like we'll have to be in much of a hurry, does it?"

Smith responded with a chuckle of his own. "Right you are, Payne. I won't be going anywhere for a while, it seems, so why not? But you'd better pull up a couple of those crates over there by the wall and get comfortable. I'm afraid this could take quite some time!"

Geoffry and Billy hauled the boxes over to the cell door and sat down. "Now then," Geoffry encouraged, "can you tell us just what *happened* after Wawoka led the three of you off into the woods?"

Captain Smith reached into his pocket, producing a short pipe and a pouch of Indian tobacco. "Gifts from Powhatan," he explained. He looked around. "But wait a minute, I guess they won't actually do me much good in here, will they, since there's no campfire or fireplace to provide a light in these grand accommodations." He chuckled again, returning the items to his pocket. "Now, how I got these, and how I got back to the fort is a story you'll find hard to believe. But it's the truth, so help me. You'll just have to take my word for it."

The two listeners nodded, wide-eyed, inviting the Captain to go ahead. "Well, it was like this, men: When Wawoka took us off through the woods, he indicated we were headed for a village called Werowaconoco, where Powhatan lived ~ his base of operations as werowance, or chief, over the whole area.

"Everything went along fine until the second day, when we got to the territory of the Pamunkeys ~ Wawoka's own tribe and one of the many in Powhatan's Confederation. Wawoka warned us to be careful, even though the Pamunkeys are supposedly allies of the big chief, and sure enough he was right. Despite our caution and Wawoka's presence, we were attacked by a band of warriors, and I tell you, they knew how to fight! That's when our two companions were killed, in spite of their muskets and training."

Smith hesitated, evidently still pained by the thought, until Billy broke in, "But what about *you*, Cap'n? How did ya get captured, an' all? How come *you* wasn't killed, like them others?"

The Captain laughed and went on, "That's one of the more interesting parts of the story, Bascomb. Oh, I put up a pretty good fight, all right, and actually ran two of their warriors through with my sword. But there were just too many of them, and finally they jumped me. I'm sure they planned to kill me right off. In fact, they tied me to a tree, though not too tight, and then they started dancing around me, waving their weapons and screaming loud enough to wake the dead. I think they were trying to scare me, to see if I'd beg for mercy first. Well, I just kept talking and talking to them instead, in a nice calm voice, even though I knew they probably didn't understand a word of what I was saying.

"Finally I remembered the little compass I always carry in my pocket, and I managed to reach down and get it out to show them. You should have seen them! They couldn't figure out how that tiny needle always kept pointing in the same direction, no matter which way I turned the compass. They tried to stop it, but of course they couldn't because of the glass. It was really kind of comical! Anyway, it must have made them think it was some kind of magic, that I was someone pretty powerful. So instead of killing me, they decided to take me as a prize right to the big chief himself, to Powhatan ~ which is exactly where I wanted to go in the first place!" Smith grinned at the recollection.

His two listeners looked on in awe, unsure what to make of such a fanciful tale. "What was Powhatan like, sir?" Geoffry wanted to know. "Did he just let you *go?*"

"Oh no, I wasn't out of trouble yet, not at all. You see, Chief Powhatan was just as angry as the Pamunkey's because I'd killed those two warriors. They were his allies, remember, and he planned to make me pay and pay dearly. In fact, he sentenced me to death."

It was too much for Billy. "But you're *here,* Cap'n! You ain't killed at all! So how on God's green earth did ya…"

Smith interrupted with a broad smile: "Patience, Bascomb, patience. I *told* you this was a long story. And the most unbelievable part is still to come."

He waited until Geoffry and Billy both settled back, then went on: "It seems that Powhatan's people have a traditional way of executing their enemies. It's pretty simple, really. They just tie the prisoner up, put his head on a big rock, and then bash his brains out with a huge club. It's not only simple but very effective and very permanent, wouldn't you say? So that's what they decided to do to me."

As Billy's eyes reflected even greater curiosity, Smith held up his hand. "Let me finish! I guess you can see their system wasn't quite as effective with *me,* was it?" He laughed again at his little joke.

"But how…." Geoffry broke in.

"Like I said before, *patience,* men! I'll tell you what happened, even though I'm not sure you'll believe me. And I promise, I'm not making any of this up!

"So there I was, all tied up, my head on the ceremonial rock, with a warrior who looked as big as a tree, with arms like huge limbs and with a club to match, standing over me, ready to flatten my head. I'll have to admit, in spite of all my adventures with the Turks and with all of my lucky escapes before, I was pretty sure this time it was all over.

"You'd never, ever be able to guess who saved me, but I swear it's absolutely true. It was Chief Powhatan's daughter!"

"The chief's own *daughter?*" Geoffry was incredulous.

"Yes, his daughter, honest! Her name is Matoaka, but everyone calls her Pocahontas, the 'lively one'! She's only a child, really, maybe twelve or thirteen years old. For some reason, she seemed to have taken a liking to me or felt sorry for me or something. Anyway, at the last second, Pocahontas ran up and took my head in her arms. She used her own body to shield me from getting smashed. And since she was the daughter of the chief, the warriors didn't dare defy her. But the strange thing is, according to their customs it means that she's also now *responsible* for me ~ for the rest of my life, if you can imagine! And that's how I finally got released!"

"Blimey!" Billy could hold back no longer. "If that ain't the strangest tale what I ever heard tell in my tee-total life! Saved by a real live Indyun princess, was ya now, Cap'n? Me oh my! If that don't beat all! Sure wish I could tell all of this to my ol' Mum, I do. Woowee!"

"But where did you get all that corn?" Geoffry was still not satisfied. "And how did you get it back here to the fort? Are you sure you're telling us everything, sir?"

"Wait a minute! Wait a minute!" the Captain responded, his eyes twinkling at their consternation. "So far I've only told you the most interesting parts, to see if you'd believe me. So let me finish!"

Now Smith related how he'd been able to strike up a genuine friendship with Chief Powhatan. First he'd had to convince the chief that the English truly had come only to trade, not to steal the Indians' land ~ as was the general suspicion after the Roanoke Island disaster. After that, as a way of furthering the amicable relationship thus established, the great chief had agreed to send Smith back to the fort with Wawoka as a guide, and also to include a gift of corn for the settlers. Smith admitted that he had not told Powhatan of the desperate straits into which the settlement had descended for fear that such a sign of weakness would only encourage further attacks.

"All I can hope for now," the Captain concluded, "is that what that idiot Perliss did to Wawoka won't destroy all of my efforts. I guess we'll just have to wait and see."

The conclusion of the Captain's fanciful narrative enabled Geoffry to return to the *real* purpose of their visit: "Captain Smith, sir, after all you've been through, we can't just *leave* you here like this in this cell. It isn't fair! It wasn't your fault those two men were killed. That scum Archer is only using all of this as an excuse to get you out of the way so he can run the Council the way he wants to."

"Yeah, Cap'n. We needs to find out how we can *help* ya!" Billy looked around. "D'ya s'pose we can figger out how to orgainze some kinda jail-break or somethin'?"

Their conversation was interrupted by the guard who had earlier proved so accommodating. Now he rushed in with a dire warning: "Billy, you an' your friend best get outa here, an' *fast!* Some o' them Council members is a'comin' this way, and that'll only mean trouble for *all* of us if they catch ya in here with the Cap'n!"

Geoffry looked around frantically. He saw that the only available avenue of escape was through the heavy guardhouse door, the door that the Council members were now approaching. Could there be some corner, some crevice, any place at *all* that could offer concealment? He saw nothing. As the voices outside reached the door, Geoffry grabbed the crate upon which he had been sitting and urged in a hushed tone, "*Quick*, Billy, drag your crate back over there by the wall, where it's darker!" Both men moved as fast as they could. "Tip it up, Billy, and get underneath!"

Slowly the door swung open and the Council members filed in. In the dim light, no one was visible except the guard and, in his cell, Captain Smith.

Gabriel Archer barely glanced around before marching ceremoniously to the little cell to confront its occupant. "Well, Smith, we meet again. We certainly hope you're enjoying our hospitality and our fine accommodations here." His eyes swept briefly around the area, and he smirked: "But please don't get too comfortable, you hear? The Council of Virginia has agreed to accept my recommendation, which is this: you are hereby sentenced to be *hanged*." He paused for dramatic effect, then continued, "After all, it was your rank incompetence that led to the deaths of those two fine men. That is equivalent to committing murder! And it is our unanimous opinion that you must now pay the ultimate penalty for your negligence."

Archer seemed somewhat disappointed at Captain Smith's lack of response. Still, he appeared to relish greatly his role in making the announcement, and concluded smugly, "Enjoy your final night with us, Smith. We'll all be back to see you in the morning, one last time!"

Chapter 14

Once the haughty visitors had gone, Geoffry and Billy crept from beneath their crates. "Did ya hear that, mate? Did ya, now? They's plannin' to *hang* the Cap'n, they are! What're we gonna *do*?"

"We'll have to figure out *something*, Billy. There's no way we can let that bunch get away with stupidity like that! Let's see if Captain Smith has any ideas."

Smith seemed far less impressed with the dangers posed by the vengeful Council than were Geoffry and Billy. "Don't worry about me, men. They've threatened to hang me before, remember? And I'm still here, as you can plainly see." He chuckled. "Go get some sleep now, and we'll see what tomorrow brings." In a more serious vein, he added, "I *do* appreciate your concerns, though. You two are good men. Too bad there aren't a few like you on that dim-witted Council."

It proved to be a restless, largely sleepless night for Geoffry. Early the next morning he was up and about, still trying desperately to conjure up some plan, some course of action by which he could aid Captain Smith. Leaving their still-uncompleted quarters, he proceeded on outside the fort to walk along the James River, hoping the clear pre-dawn air might stimulate his thinking more effectively.

As the sun's first rays broke softly over the distant horizon, the spreading light revealed something far more significant than just the new day. Geoffry was certain he detected a faint movement far down-river ~ a hint of something white emerging from the low-hanging mists that still enshrouded the water. He strained to see more clearly. Could it *be*? With surging euphoria born of buoyant hope, yet tempered by dread that he might be wrong, he watched, hardly daring to believe the possibility of such great good fortune!

Then as the rising sun burned away the last lingering wisps of haze, he saw that it was actually *true*! Moving slowly, steadily ~ *majestically*, it appeared to Geoffry ~ up the river toward James Fort was a ship, its white canvass sails unfurled, proudly flying the Union Jack. It could be none other than the long-anticipated supply vessel bringing provisions from England, provisions that were *crucial* to the colony's survival! And even more significant, in Geoffry's mind, it meant that Captain Christopher Newport had returned ~ Newport, friend and protector of Captain John Smith!

Unable to contain himself, Geoffry sprinted back through the gates of the fort, shouting at the top of his lungs, "A ship! A ship! A ship's coming up the James! It might be Captain Newport!"

A few early risers were straggling around the settlement ~ some working to start cooking fires, others going about everyday chores. At Geoffry's outcry, they headed immediately for the river to see for themselves what was going on, adding their voices to the general din as they ran. In a few minutes, it seemed, the entire encampment was alive and bustling, creating a scene of near pandemonium as all raced to greet the long-awaited arrival.

When Geoffry got back to their unfinished shelter, he found a still sleep-befuddled Billy emerging uncertainly to see what all the commotion was about. "Come on, Billy!" Geoffry yelled. "There's a ship coming up the James! Hurry up, let's go find out what's happening!"

As the two joined the disorderly rush to the river, Geoffry added, "I think it could be Captain Newport, Billy, back with those supplies! I really, really hope so! He might be able to get Captain Smith out of that jail, if *anyone* can!"

"Right ya are, mate," Billy agreed as realization dawned. "Right ya are! Remember, he got the Cap'n freed once before, he did! And I'll just betcha he can do 'er again! Oh yeah!"

The supply ship continued its steady progress toward the fort, buoyed by the hurrahs and cheers of the ecstatic colonists. When at last it anchored and was secured to the dock, first to descend the gangplank was Captain Newport, resplendent in his distinctive uniform, smiling broadly, waving to the motley group assembled. It was all that was left by now of England's "grand experiment."

First in line to greet the Captain were members of the Council of Virginia, with Gabriel Archer at their head. After the customary exchange of salutations and pleasantries, the Captain scanned the waiting crowd, then inquired, "And where's Captain Smith? Why isn't he present? Is he not well?"

Archer related with obvious relish the circumstances that had led to Smith's arrest and incarceration, utilizing the most damaging language and descriptions possible. He finished his report with a slight bow and added with a note of self-righteousness, "The decision of the Council was unanimous."

The barrister, mindful only of his own devious goals and objectives, could in no way have anticipated the Captain's reaction to this news. Now Archer, along with the fawning cohorts who huddled around him nodding sanctimonious assent, found themselves recipients of Captain Newport's unmitigated, unrelenting wrath. There was no longer any hint of deference or of intimidation due to the elevated "status" of the Council members as the Captain thundered loudly and forcefully, "You fools have done *what*? Placed Captain Smith in the *guardhouse*? Well, let me tell you what *my* 'unanimous decision' is, you bunch of supercilious popinjays! It is that you are without doubt the most idiotic, addlepated, dim-witted collection of imbeciles I have ever laid eyes on! Now, you listen to *me!* You will all march 'unanimously' to that guardhouse this instant, and you will 'unanimously' <u>release</u> Captain Smith! **Immediately!** *Is that clear?*"

"But Captain Newport," Gabriel Archer protested with attempted bravado, "the Council's decision…"

For a moment it appeared to Geoffry that the irate Captain might actually strike the simpering lawyer in his rage. Slowly, however, he regained his composure, drew back, and took a deep breath. "You heard my order! You *will* release Captain Smith, *at once*! I said, **at once**!"

There was absolutely no room for argument. Meekly, despite muted muttering and grumbling, the Council members shuffled off toward the guardhouse, where Archer ordered the guard to unlock the cell door. The guard tried hard to hide his jubilant smile, but without success.

John Smith stepped out of his cell, looking as though he fully expected that the Council had come to carry out its previous decision regarding his execution. Then his glance fell on Captain Newport, and he stopped short.

"Why, welcome back, Captain! We've all been anxiously awaiting your return, to say the least." Again he looked around. "Am I to understand that you are in agreement with the sentence imposed by our illustrious Council?"

"Quite the contrary, Captain Smith. I have come to oversee your *release!* My only hope is that you will now resume your capable work in helping to put this settlement back on a sound basis….that is," Newport looked around menacingly at the subdued members of the Council, "if you can forgive the sheer *stupidity* exhibited by some of its so-called leaders."

A wide grin spread across Smith's face. He stepped forward to grasp Captain Newport's hand. "Thank you, Captain, thank you very much! Please feel free to continue to call upon me for *any* assistance, whatever the need may be." With that, he clapped Newport on the back and the two strolled off together, deep in animated conversation.

"Well, I never!" sniffed Archer. "Of all the impudence! These pretentious military types just don't understand how proper society operates." Sweeping his brocaded cape around his shoulders, he stalked out of the guardhouse, his sycophants traipsing after.

Geoffry and Billy made no effort to hide their joy. Once the Council members were out of sight, Billy grabbed his friend jubilantly by both arms and swung him into a lively jig, laughing uproariously as they twirled about. "Now ain't that just somethin' else, mate?" Billy crowed. "Good ol' Cap'n Newport, showin' up like that, just in the nick o' time, an' all! Woowee!!"

Geoffry's elation matched that of his companion: "You're absolutely right, Billy! Who could've guessed? And did you see the faces of those Council members? Especially Archer's?" The thought brought a renewed burst of merriment from both men.

"Looks like ol' Archer's gonna have to learn how to get along with Cap'n Smith after all, don't it? Me oh my! Ain't this just the *bestest?*"

The exultant pair finally made their way back toward the dock, where they were soon engaged in helping to unload the stock of new supplies and transporting the goods to the storehouse. In the process, they also had opportunity to meet and chat with a few of the newcomers who had come along on the supply ship. From them they gleaned a hint of the great sense of nationalistic pride, the excitement back home in "Mother England" at the prospect that this first extension of English domination, English culture, into the wilds of the New World might yet succeed!

Altogether, Geoffry and Billy agreed as they returned to their quarters, it had been a good day. Not only had Captain Smith been saved from the gallows, he was going to continue in his role of leadership, thereby helping to insure that the little colony was at least likely to survive if not prosper. And with the addition of both fresh supplies and fresh manpower, the two men felt encouraged that prospects for the future of their settlement here in the wilderness did now appear much brighter.

Chapter 15

In the days that followed, Geoffry came to believe more and more that his long-held optimism about the future of their "grand experiment" might at last prove justified. There was a new burst of energy and enthusiasm in the air as Captain Newport, assisted by Captain Smith, directed repairs still needed on the fire-damaged fort. Furthermore, Geoffry sensed that longer-range plans were beginning to take shape ~ plans that went well beyond the original dreams of instant acquisition of wealth. It would require a great deal of hard work and cooperation, he knew, but the possibility that the settlement might finally become a *permanent* establishment, an actual "new home," seemed to be emerging. An air of confidence, almost a "proprietary" feeling, was developing regarding this new country ~ an attitude that up to now had been sadly lacking.

Part of the change may have come about, Geoffry thought, when Captain Newport reported on the load of stones he had taken back to England to be assayed for gold. A careful evaluation of this "ore" had revealed that it had absolutely *no* mineral value whatsoever, that the colonists had sent over nothing more than a load of worthless "fool's gold."

As this reality began to sink in, the disillusioned former gold-seekers appeared to come to a new realization: perhaps the wealth of this New World lay *not* in easy access to instant riches such as gold, silver, or pearls. Instead, its great prospective potential may actually be its *other* natural resources ~ plentiful timber, naval stores such as tar, pitch, rosin, and turpentine, plus iron ore and fish ~ all of which could serve as the basis for a flourishing *trade* with "Mother England."

Beyond the resources, Geoffry saw something more: almost limitless prospects offered by the vast tracts of available <u>land</u> in Virginia. With diligent effort, he was convinced that the rich soil could be utilized to raise vital food crops, with ample surpluses left over to send back to England in exchange for essential manufactured goods. And as he envisioned the endless acres coming under cultivation, Geoffry had a *further* insight: was it out of the realm of possibility, he wondered, that at some future date this new land might actually produce not only excess raw materials and food, but develop its *own* base of industry and manufacturing as well? If so, might that not enable the colony to actually become *totally self-sufficient*, no longer dependent upon "Mother England" *at all?* It was a mind-boggling concept, almost too grandiose to comprehend!

The scarcity of land for farming back home in England, Geoffry well understood from his experiences in the Salisbury region, had created upheaval and distress for a segment of society that was growing constantly larger. As English factories began to take worldwide precedence in the production of woolen cloth, that rise had been accompanied by an ever-increasing demand for more raw wool. This, in turn, led to thousands of small farmers, especially those barely existing on rented land, being forced off their farms so that land could be utilized instead as pasturage for wool-producing sheep. Displaced farmers drifted to the cities in hopes of finding employment, adding to increased demands for urban housing and other social services. Unmet needs created a volatile, dangerous atmosphere, so tense that some in authority feared actual revolution.

The solution, the authorities seemed to conclude, lay in relieving these pressures through colonization *outside* the homeland. If enough of this "excess population," especially the unemployed, could be persuaded to migrate to the New World, it might serve as a "safety valve" that would remove the immediate threat posed by the discontented. All that was needed was a campaign to spread word of the glorious opportunities available in the New World "paradise" for those willing to face its risks. And if Mother England benefited economically in the process ~ well, so much the better!

Geoffrey remembered vividly the appearance of endless pamphlets, articles, and "broadsides" extolling the virtues of the exotic new land that lay across the Atlantic. He was certain that, whether directly or subliminally, this propaganda had helped to influence his *own* thinking. After all, here he was ~ in a totally new environment, part of a "grand experiment," captivated by the potential that lay all about him!

He was encouraged by the fact that, since Captain John Smith's release from prison and return to authority, discipline and order had again been restored to the faltering James Fort colony. Work parties were organized to build a blockhouse where their peninsula met the mainland, providing added protection against surprise attack. Smith also established a system of military drill, with a rotating force set up to stand watch, all under his own watchful and vigilant scrutiny.

With the colony settling into a more stable routine, Captain Smith appeared to feel free to follow up his earlier explorations of the surrounding countryside. Impetus for these excursions was furthered by persistent rumors that there were rich copper mines nearby, believed to be controlled by a tribe called the Mandoags. Additional motivation came from reported sightings amongst these natives of persons dressed not in traditional native attire, but rather wearing clothing made in typical *English* styles.

Unfortunately, just as before, the Captain's forays yielded neither copper nor gold nor the elusive passage to the South Seas nor any contacts with possible survivors of the ill-fated "Lost Colony." However, Smith's continuing friendship with Powhatan *did* result in an alliance with the influential chief that brought not only a welcome period of peace but ongoing trade with the native population for needed provisions.

Geoffry and Billy Bascomb entered whole-heartedly into the new activities, happy that Captain Smith was once again in control and providing a sense of organization and direction. After each day's chores, the pair returned to work on their own little dwelling, now nearing completion. And it was here that Geoffry was able to call once again upon those skills he had acquired back home in Salisbury as a stone-worker.

"Hey, Billy," he suggested to his partner one day, "I really don't think we have to be satisfied to live in a house with just a plain old dirt floor. Makes it awfully hard to keep things clean."

"That it does, mate, that it does. So what do ya have in mind? Ya want I should run down to the corner market and buy ya a *marble* floor, do ya now?"

Geoffry responded with a laugh. "Well, go right ahead, if you can find one about twelve feet by twenty or thereabouts." Then he laid out his proposal. "This is what I was thinking, Billy: I noticed there's a lot of loose shale rock at different places down along the river. Now I realize it would mean extra work, but if we were to haul some of that shale back here to our cabin, I think I could lay out a pretty nice stone floor for this place."

"Could ya now? Well, I just bet ya could at that, I do! And I'm right willin' to try to help, I am. What say, mate, let's give 'er a go!"

Together they began transporting pieces of the flat stone back to their shelter, piling them in a corner out of the way. Each evening Geoffry worked at setting the pieces in place ~ scraping dirt, leveling, packing. Before long, an attractive and serviceable stone floor covered the entire interior of their shelter.

"What do you think, Billy?" Geoffry asked as he stepped back to survey his handiwork. He had used the variety of shades and colors in the different stones to advantage, creating an attractive random pattern that could have graced any English country estate.

Billy was obviously impressed. "Why, I think it looks just *grand*, it does, mate, an' that's a fact! It surely does!" He studied the workmanship as though in awe, then mused, "Just wish my ol' Mum back home could o' had somethin' half as fine, I do. Yesiree. Ya done right good, mate, ya truly did!"

Geoffry laughed, pleased at the high praise. "Well, if this floor meets your approval, Billy, I've got *another* idea, for later on."

"Yeah? An' what might that be?"

"Maybe later, when we have more time, we can gather up some of those stones the men keep digging out of the fields out there and I can build us a proper fireplace. You know, for cooking and heating and such, like back home. Those 'wattle and daub' chimneys seem to catch fire pretty easily. And we don't want the whole fort to burn down again, now do we?"

"My, my, if you don't beat all, mate! Yesiree! And I just bet ya can do 'er, too, ya can. Ya do beat all!"

Their self-congratulatory mood was interrupted by the intrusion of an unmistakably familiar, unpleasant, and unwelcome voice: "Ah, so *this* is where th' two o' ya hangs out, is it? Well, well! Tha's good ta know, Payne...." Pike Perliss's swarthy face appeared in the doorway. With slow, deliberate movements, he shuffled into the room. His right hand protruded from a makeshift sling, part of the ragged wrap that still encased his ribcage. "An' reme'mer, Payne, I ain't forgot what ya done ta me, neither! Nosiree! Ol' Pike never fergits *nothin,'* he don't! You'll git yers, jist wait an' ...."

He halted momentarily, his beady eyes sweeping the interior of the cabin. For just an instant, the eyes widened in a look of surprise and admiration. This passed quickly, however, replaced by a flash of envy and followed by the customary sneer. "Oh, an' I s'pose ya thinks this here's somethin' special, does ya? Ha! Well, *anybody* kin lay out a floor like this'n, they can, if'n they on'y wants ta. I knows *I* could! Anyways, this here ain't near *half* sa fine as what we gots in our place back home, it ain't. This here ain't *nothin'!*" With a final defiant glance at Geoffry's handiwork, Pike turned, grimacing with the effort, and stalked off.

Geoffry and Billy looked at each other for a moment, not sure what to make of the rude intrusion but fully aware of the dangers posed by Pike Perliss's antagonism. Gradually, Geoffry's face creased in a wide grin. "Well Billy, it's nice to know our floor meets Pike's discriminating approval, isn't it? But I'm still not sure we'll want to invite him to our 'housewarming'."

Billy responded with a loud guffaw. "Yeah, mate, maybe we should o' invited 'im to stay for tea or somethin,' shouldn't we now? My, my! We's surely forgettin' our manners, ain't we though?" After another burst of laughter, he added in a serious tone, "But we *do* hafta take any threats from ol' Pike serious, we does, mate. He's downright mean, he is, an' that's a fact!"

"Just the same Pike Perliss he's always been, Billy. Never seems to know when to quit, does he? I guess about all we can do is stay alert and keep a sharp eye out for him. But remember, we can't let him keep us from doing what needs to be done, either."

With James Fort now bustling from all of the newly instituted activities, Captain Newport determined to return once more to England to procure ever-needed supplies. Fortunately, at least in Geoffry's estimation, Newport took with him several members of the Council of Virginia, including the troublesome attorney Gabriel Archer.

Inexplicably, however, when the Captain returned some months later, his cargo did not include the expected provisions. Instead, he brought with him seventy new settlers, including the usual allotment of "gentlemen." Interspersed among the rest of the group, however, were several colonists who proved to be most welcome additions: they actually possessed true skills as craftsmen. Included were some Dutch and Polish immigrants found to be proficient in producing pitch, tar, and potash, while others had at least a rudimentary knowledge of glassmaking.

It did not take long for the determined Captain John Smith to put the skills of these new charges to good use. With Gabriel Archer no longer present to oppose him, Smith managed to get himself elected President of the Council of Virginia, and he was able to use this new authority effectively to try to ensure that the "grand experiment" would not fail. Once more his previous edict went into effect, applying to all equally and without exception: "He that will not work, shall not eat!"

Through utilization of this vital leverage, and with the assistance of the newly-arrived craftsmen, the settlement soon began to generate new products suitable for export back to the mother country. The skilled workmen established a simple glass works, turning out panes of crude but serviceable glass. Others labored at digging and smelting iron ore, found to be much more readily available than the elusive gold still coveted by a number of the colonists and by the

London Company. Small quantities of naval stores such as pine pitch and tar were prepared for export, to be used by the Royal Navy. Fire-pits fueled with wood procured from the bountiful forests yielded ash, essential both for making soap to wash the huge quantities of wool being produced in England and as a basic ingredient in the glass-making process.

Settlers were also put to work clearing land *outside* the walls of James Fort, and crops of corn were planted in the hill-manner adopted from the natives. Other colonists hunted wild ducks and geese in the swamps, fished for sturgeon in the James River, or gathered oysters along its banks. Pigs and chickens were allowed to roam freely on a nearby island where they could forage for food and increase in numbers.

The result was that, as the days went by, the settlement seemed to be moving *past* the stage of mere "existence." Beyond the confines of the original fort enclosure, twenty or more huts and shelters gradually emerged in random fashion along makeshift "streets." A new well provided safe drinking water. Even the little church that had been destroyed in the ruinous fire that had struck the fort was now rebuilt.

As he led a work party to its assigned tasks one day, Captain Smith stopped to survey the growing array of structures. Turning to Geoffry and Billy Bascomb, he observed with obvious satisfaction, "You know, men, if this kind of building keeps on, before long it will be time to change the name of our little settlement here from James Fort to *James' Towne,* won't it?"

"Right you are, sir," Geoffry agreed. "And that has a nice ring to it, too, doesn't it? More of a sound of *permanence!* Maybe it will help encourage more settlers to come over and join us."

There did indeed appear to be justification for a new attitude of optimism and hope ~ hope that the straggling little colony might at last be ready to move beyond mere survival toward actual prosperity. The difficulties and trials of establishing their fragile, tenuous foothold in the wilderness finally appeared to have become merely a condition of the past.

Chapter 16

▼

Unfortunately for the settlers at "James' Towne," the days and weeks that followed brought a relentless chain of events whose cumulative effect was to bring with it a systematic erosion of all of Geoffry's high hopes and dreams. The process began innocently enough, with circumstances no one could have foreseen or foretold. Still, the aftermath was to leave him in disillusion and despair, with the haunting realization that it would be almost a miracle if their little colony managed to survive at all.

The troubles started when a new aggregation of colonists descended upon James' Towne, part of what came to be known as the "Third Supply." But these colonists were only the unfortunate "end result" of basic and far-reaching changes that had taken place back in England long before their arrival ~ changes instituted at the direction of the London Company.

As the newcomers explained upon their arrival, the London Company had finally had its fill with the bickering and feuding of the Council of Virginia. Accordingly, the Company directors had drawn up a new charter for their Virginia endeavor, relegating the old Council to a mere "advisory" role and replacing it with a "governor-for-life" of their own choosing. In *his* hands would be vested ultimate authority over the daily functions and operations of the colony. To fill this august position, the Company selected Sir Thomas West, Lord De La Warr. To assist him, they chose Sir Thomas Gates to serve as Lieutenant Governor.

Next, the London Company decreed that henceforth immigrants sent to Virginia would no longer include in their numbers "gentlemen" seeking merely to regain lost fortunes. Rather, colonists would be individuals who could ensure steady *profitable returns* for the Company: fishermen, metal workers, weavers, brick-makers, shoemakers, sawyers. Others sent to provide both stability and security for the venture would include hunters, bakers, even architects to design proper English dwellings.

Problems arose when the Company sought to *recruit* qualified settlers such as these. The directors soon found there simply weren't enough skilled laborers *willing to risk* their entire futures on an uncertain "roll of the dice" like migrating to Virginia. Therefore, the directors were forced to accept instead as "craftsmen" large numbers of persons generally classed as "excess population" ~ poor unemployed unfortunates huddled in the teeming slums of London, including a goodly number of cut-throats, thieves, renegades, thugs, and all-around "riff-raff." But as later events were to prove, the make-up and background of this group was only the *beginning* of the difficulties encountered by this "Third Supply."

Altogether, the London Company managed to outfit and supply a much larger contingent than usual: a total of nine ships, designed to transport about five hundred settlers. With Governor De La Warr remaining behind in England for the time, the fleet set out in June of 1609 under the command of Sir Thomas Gates. As it turned out, the crossing proved to be anything but "routine," since in the stormy Atlantic the fleet soon found itself caught in the midst of a fearsome hurricane.

Thus it was not until August that seven battered ships finally limped up to the dock at James' Towne, some having lost even their mainmasts during the perilous passage. As related by the survivors, one ship had foundered and sunk during the wild tempest. Another, the one carrying Lieutenant-Governor Gates, was believed to have been wrecked on the shores of Bermuda. Among those individuals who *did* manage to survive the harrowing crossing was none other than the proverbial "bad penny" ~ Captain John Smith's old protagonist, Gabriel Archer.

This sudden influx of several hundred new settlers, many ill and totally lacking in provisions, taxed the resources of the struggling colony to the breaking point. The sole redeeming factor was that, since neither the appointed Governor De La Warr nor Lieutenant Governor Gates had yet arrived, in their absence Captain John Smith insisted on retaining his position as President of the Council of Virginia. Despite Archer's strenuous objections, Smith was able to continue enforcing at least a modicum of order and discipline on the motley, unruly conglomeration.

Then the *final* catastrophe struck.

It started when Captain Smith ventured forth once again on a journey of exploration, searching for additional sources of supplies. This time, as he reported upon his return, his excursion took him far up the James River, past the barrier of waterfalls and on to the hilly regions beyond. It was here, as he and his party spent a quiet evening in their tent, that the accident occurred.

As the Captain told the story later, he had been cleaning and checking his weapon, making sure it was in prime condition for instant use should that become necessary. But while he was measuring out a paper of powder, a random spark from their campfire somehow ignited his entire *horn* of gunpowder. A violent explosion ensued. When the smoke cleared, Captain Smith was found to have sustained a severe, excruciating wound to his thigh.

Despite the agony and discomfort, Smith refused assistance on the return trip. But by the time the party again reached James' Towne, the Captain was no longer able to conceal the torment he was suffering. When Geoffry and Billy Bascomb stopped by his quarters to wish him well, they could see immediately that there was no way Smith would be able to carry on his duties. The drawn face, the feverish eyes, the spasms of pain brought on by any movement, told more eloquently than words what misery the Captain was enduring.

"We're truly sorry about your accident, sir," Geoffry began.

"That we are, Cap'n, that we are, an' no mistake!" Billy chimed in.

"Is there anything at all we can *do* to help, sir? *Anything?*"

Captain Smith peered at the two anxious faces through eyes half-shut with anguish. "Like I've said before, you two are good men," he responded, almost in a whisper. "I'm just not sure that *anyone* can do much to help right now. This thing will take time to heal, that's all. But I'll be back on my feet before you know it, just wait and see!"

"We knows ya will, Cap'n, we surely do! If them there Turks an' all couldn't stop ya, why, a little ol' leg wound won't neither. We just *knows* you'll be alright, an' that's a fact!"

A wan smile creased the Captain's face, despite his tightly-clenched teeth. The eyes softened a bit. "Thanks, Bascomb. And you too, Payne. If we just had a few more like the two of you around here, I'd feel a whole lot better about being shipped back to England."

Looks of surprise and consternation greeted this news. "Shipped back to England? What do you mean, sir? You can't be serious!"

Captain Smith lifted his hand in a feeble gesture. "It's all right, men, it's all right! Perhaps the Council knows best, and I really *do* need proper medical care from a qualified physician. Anyway, that's what they've decided, in spite of all my protests."

"But *why*, Cap'n? Why can't ya just stay here, like always? Me an' Geoffry can look after ya, we can, good as any o' them fancy doctors back in England. Maybe *better*, even!"

"We'd be *happy* to try to take care of you, sir, if that's what you'd like. Billy, here, is just *full* of remedies he's learned from his good old Mum."

The Captain could only smile weakly at their concern. "Thank you, men, thank you kindly for what you're trying to do. But I'm afraid the decision is out of my hands." He paused briefly, then added, "I hope they're not just trying to get rid of me, though, so they can manipulate things their own way here while I'm gone. I wouldn't put anything past that scoundrel Archer."

Geoffry grimaced at mention of the despicable lawyer. "You may be right, sir. That hypocrite is capable of almost *anything!* And we thought we'd finally got rid of him when he went back home with Captain Newport. But oh, no! Not Archer! Here he is back again, and more trouble than ever!"

"Yeah, too bad *he* couldn't o' drownded, 'stead o' some o' them *other* poor blokes what died in the shipwreck, ain't it now? But not ol' Archer! He just had to survive somehow, like the rat he is."

"Now, now, men. You'll be just fine, I'm sure. Maybe I'll be able to get back here quicker than expected, if I can only heal up fast enough."

As had been feared, the vengeful Council made certain that Captain Smith was hustled aboard the very first ship to leave James Towne, sent on his way back home to "recuperate." To take Smith's place as head of the settlement, the Council turned to one of its colleagues, George Percy, known to be totally weak and indecisive and thus a much easier pawn to control than John Smith had proved to be.

And with the feisty Captain's departure, it was not long before Geoffry's worst fears began to be realized. In fact, those fears were soon dramatically and drastically *exceeded!*

Chapter 17

▼

With Captain Smith no longer present to impose his iron rule, the enforced discipline that had brought about James' Towne's evolving stability evaporated like a morning mist. Willful settlers acted as though they had been relieved of some great burden, and were now finally free to pursue their *own* best interests. Some returned to their vain search for gold, apparently still certain that it lay somewhere within easy reach. "Gentlemen" who had been forced to work alongside laborers returned to their previous leisurely pursuits. Crops went untended, and the animals set aside to produce flocks or herds for the benefit of the community were quickly slaughtered and consumed.

Watching the disintegration, Geoffry could scarcely contain his frustration and indignation. "Just *look* at those lazy sots," he fumed to Billy. "Not doing a thing, wasting their time like they expected King James himself to come riding in to wait on them."

"Right ya are, mate. The worthless rubbish! Cap'n Smith would be havin' a apoplexy fit if he could see 'em, wouldn't he now?"

It didn't take long for the dire effects of such indolence to manifest itself. Shortages of food and supplies led to incessant bickering. Rather than forage in the woods for nuts, berries, or edible plants, colonists seemed to put all of their efforts into trying to obtain a larger portion than their neighbors of the dwindling resources still available. Such "dog-eat-dog" tactics resulted naturally in retaliatory actions on the part of those who now felt wronged. Cooperative attempts to solve common problems became totally non-existent, and as a result, an already desperate situation grew worse by the day.

Adding to the accumulating problems was an adverse weather pattern: the colony appeared to be in the throes of a prolonged drought. The acute lack of precipitation hindered even further the few feeble efforts to produce food in the small garden plots. Both Geoffry and Billy were puzzled by the shortage of rainfall, especially as compared to what they had been accustomed to back in England.

"Blimey, mate, do ya s'pose it don't *never* rain here *a'tall?* This sure ain't nothin' like back home anyway, it ain't. Seems like it's been *forever* since we had us a proper rain, don't it?"

"You're right about that, Billy. We've had us a really long dry spell, haven't we? Maybe we just don't know what to expect. But with all of the trees and vegetation around here, there *must* normally be more rain than this."

"Do ya s'pose we could be gettin' punished for our 'wicked ways,' like happened in some o' them stories in the Good Book what my Mum used to read to me?"

"No, I really don't think so, Billy. I don't think God operates like that. It's probably just one of nature's cycles. But like you said, it sure seems to be lasting an extra long time!"

Without replenishing rain, the shallow wells that had been dug to provide safe drinking water began to go dry. Rather than put forth the effort required to deepen the wells or search for fresh springs, many colonists turned to their old practice of obtaining drinking water from the James River. But as before, the intrusion of salt water forced inland by the ocean tides rendered this a less-than-desirable solution. The swampy areas left behind as the tides receded also yielded only the usual brackish, stagnant pools ~ polluted waters that soon proved to be havens for breeding millions of malaria-bearing mosquitoes. The spread of various diseases again reached epidemic proportions.

Billy Bascomb provided a bit of "folk wisdom" that might have aided in relieving the danger, had anyone bothered to listen to his advice. Only Geoffry seemed persuaded that there was merit in what Billy suggested: "Back home, whenever the water from our ol' town well got to tastin' real nasty, my Mum used to *boil* it a'fore we drank it. She said she was purifyin' it, she did. And ya know, it did seem to help! Why don't we try doin' that with our river water?" Despite the extra effort involved, the two followed the regimen faithfully.

But the scarcity of food remained a constant, ever-increasing hazard, only worsened by the latest influx of immigrants. Ill-prepared to cope with the rigors of life in the wilderness, the newcomers reverted quickly to patterns of behavior learned in the London slums, not constrained by any niceties or social rules.

Their sole impulse appeared to be personal survival, as reflected in the old axiom: "The devil take the hindmost."

First they broke into the communal storehouse, despite the feeble efforts of the ineffectual guards. But even here it appeared that fate was against the colonists, since what little grain remained had been fouled by an infestation of rodents. Still, the thieves quickly appropriated everything that was left. Next they swarmed over the straggling rows of corn out in the fields, stripping the still-unripe ears from their stalks, thus eliminating all hope of a harvest that might have provided some relief. In an attempt to stem these illegal actions and perhaps at the same time bolster his dwindling authority, Council President Percy finally decreed that henceforth any person caught in the act of thievery would be executed. To set an "example," he actually sentenced several of those apprehended to be hanged ~ with no noticeable impact on solving the basic problems.

During these turbulent days, Geoffry and Billy managed to survive due largely to Billy's expertise in setting snares for small game. Both men also searched diligently in the woods for edible plants and fruit. It was while on such a foray one day that they became involved in a truly frightening encounter: a party of Indian warriors, their faces and bodies painted in terrifying fashion, materialized silently from the surrounding forest and encircled the startled pair. With menacing gestures, the warriors made it clear they *opposed* such intrusions into their territory by white settlers. Geoffry recognized, with a sense of deep regret, the *change* that had gradually taken place: more and more, distrust and hostility had by now replaced the atmosphere of friendship so carefully nurtured by Captain Smith.

"Hey mate, them natives looks downright unneighborly, they does, as if maybe they'd enjoy slicin' us up for dinner!" Billy observed, glancing from face to face. "What do ya s'pose we oughta do?"

"Just don't make any quick moves, and keep smiling," Geoffry advised, raising his left hand in the traditional sign of peace.

The leader of the group strode forward until he stood a scant few feet from Geoffry. Furious eyes peered closely into Geoffry's face, scrutinizing every feature, every detail. Billy tensed, holding his breath, ready to jump to the aid of his partner even though he knew resistance against such odds would be clearly hopeless.

The tension held for long seconds ~ seconds that seemed like hours to the two threatened companions. Then the leader stepped back, his belligerent demeanor dissolving into relaxation. Raising his left hand to mirror Geoffry's signal, and with just the hint of a smile creeping across his bronzed face, he uttered a single word: "Wawoka!"

"You know *Wawoka?*" Geoffry responded, delighted to hear a name not heard since Wawoka's unfortunate encounter with Pike Perliss. "Wawoka! Wawoka my *friend*," he concluded, grinning as he tapped his chest.

The native hesitated. Then slowly his face also lit in a broad smile. Turning to his companions, he pointed to Geoffry while tapping his own chest and repeated, "Wawoka *friend!*"

The pronouncement was received with obvious relief and pleasure, for now the entire party gathered closely around Geoffry and Billy, happily tapping their chests and patting the two men on their backs while echoing their leader: "Wawoka friend! Wawoka friend!" With a few final nods and waves of the hand, the warriors faded quietly back into the woods.

"Well now, mate, what do ya make o' all *that?*" Billy blurted out. "Me oh my! That was downright *scary*, it was, an' that's a fact!"

"You're absolutely right, Billy! I was just *sure* we were going to be done in for a while there! I wonder what happened?"

"They surely changed their tune when they saw ya up close, they did! Blimey! Maybe they thought ya was some kind o' special white *god* or somethin'."

Geoffry broke into a laugh, both at Billy's suggestion and from release of tension. "No, I don't really suppose that was it, Billy. It did seem to have something to do with Wawoka, though, didn't it?"

"That it did, mate, that it did." He was silent for a moment, then volunteered an idea: "Hey, do ya s'pose they could o' heard from some o' them other Indyuns how it was *you* what saved Wawoka from ol' Pike's knife? And was even told just what ya look like, an' all? Could that *be?* They surely checked ya over close enough, now didn't they? Do ya think word *could* possible have got spreaded around somehow?"

"I don't know, Billy. I'm as puzzled as you are. But as long as they left us in one piece, let's be grateful! And just in case they change their minds, maybe we'd better high tail it back to the fort as quick as we can!"

"Right ya are, mate! That was *mighty* close, it surely was! So like ya says, let's not take no chances, and get on back!"

Unfortunately, the changed relationship between settlers and natives did not end as happily for other colonists who wandered into the woods in search of food. Several were killed, their mutilated bodies lashed to pikes outside the gates of the fort as an apparent warning to others. Too much deception, too much wanton destruction, too many senseless killings seemed finally to have led to a breaking point. Bitter enmity once again became the norm, as threatened settlers reciprocated with their own bloody retaliation.

Stark fear now drove those who had ventured to build shelters outside the confines of the fort to flee back within the safety of its walls. This also left the problem, however, that with the renewed hostilities, *no one* felt safe any longer to venture out to supplement their meager rations by hunting or fishing or gathering food from the forest. This led naturally to even more drastic shortages and conditions that only worsened day after day for the hungry, discouraged settlers.

Starvation now became a harsh, cruel, relentless reality. Up to this time, deaths in the settlement had occurred largely from illness or disease, aggravated by lack of a proper diet. But now the grim specter of death from starvation became a daily actuality. The number of those who succumbed on some days reached more than a score of human beings.

In desperation, in an effort to cling to life absolutely as long as possible, colonists turned to devouring anything and everything in sight: dogs, cats, rats, mice, snakes, hides, leather, tree bark ~ *anything* that might sustain life for just a little longer. When even these repugnant stores were totally exhausted, some settlers resorted to more gruesome fare: the bodies of native warriors slain in the on-going clashes between colonists and Indians. Finally they descended to the absolute abyss: bodies of their own compatriots, recently buried, were unearthed from their shallow graves and the flesh consumed.

The settlement, it appeared, had fallen to its ultimate nadir! Council President Percy, surveying the chaos that had overtaken England's "noble experiment," could only characterize the pitiful situation which surrounded him on every side, the dreadful conditions he now encountered no matter where he looked, as "the Starveing Tyme."

Chapter 18

▼

From the small shelter that was their sanctuary, Geoffry and Billy witnessed the spiraling daily downward drift of James' Towne settlement, and both were filled with dismay and indignation.

"What's *wrong* with these people?" a disgusted Geoffry erupted. "Why won't they *do* anything to help themselves ~ something other than wrecking what little chance any of us may have left to survive? There's still plenty of game in the forest and fish in the river! The Indians would probably be willing to *share*, if only we'd try *getting along* with them for a change instead of just shooting them on sight. And where's the Council? And President Percy? Why don't they take *charge* here, before it's too late?"

"I knows you're right, mate, but I ask ya: what're we gonna *do* about it? I know *we* don't wanna go back in them there woods again ourselves right now, do we? It was just a bit too scary the last time, it was! Remember?"

"But if we'd only try to *cooperate* with each other, instead of always grabbing our guns right off, couldn't we maybe *work out* our differences?"

"Like I says before, mate, I knows you're right. But it just don't seem to help none to be *right* if we're here starvin' right along with all the rest of 'em, now does it?"

Geoffry knew there was no arguing with the logic of Billy's remarks, even though his sense of helplessness only intensified. "Anyway," he finally concluded, "I'm going out to look around a bit, see if there's anything at all *anywhere* left to eat that we might have missed." With that, he headed for the door.

When Geoffry returned several hours later with only a few edible greens and some roots to show for his efforts, he was surprised to find his usually buoyant little buddy back in bed, the skimpy covers pulled up tightly around his chin. A few quick strides took Geoffrey to Billy's bedside where he looked down at the quiet face, not sure whether to be amused or anxious. "Hey, Billy, what's going on? What *is* all this? Are you just pouting in there, or is something wrong?"

Billy made an effort to smile, then tried to reassure his companion in as cheerful a voice as he could muster, "Ah, I'm just fine, I am, mate! Just a little weary's all, so I thought I might catch me a extry little nap." An involuntary shiver shook his slight body. "Seems like its awful chilly in here, though, don't it?"

A sense of foreboding surged through Geoffry. He reached out and placed his hand on Billy's forehead. "Why, no *wonder* you're feeling cold, Billy! You've got a really bad fever! You're burning up!"

"Nah, it ain't nothin,' mate. Nothin' at all! I just keep on shiverin', I do, and for no reason at all what *I* can see. But I'll be right fine soon as I rest a bit, I will, just wait an' see." His reddened eyes closed slowly.

"Here, let me get you a drink of water first. And I'll get *my* blanket to help cover you too. Then you stay right there in that bed, Billy, you hear? You've got a really high fever, no mistake!" After a few moments, during which an array of terrifying scenarios flashed through his mind ~ scenarios of what he had witnessed in the settlement all too frequently in the days just passed ~ Geoffry added gently, "Now, is there anything at all I can get for you, Billy? Anything that might make you feel a little better?"

The tired eyes came partly open. "If only my good ol' Mum could be here, mate! She'd know azzackly what to do, she would. She was a right good'un whenever I got to feelin' poorly, an' all." Billy sighed deeply as his eyes again drifted shut.

"What kinds of things would she do, Billy? What would she give you to make you feel better? Maybe *I* can do some of the same things for you."

A long silence followed. Then a slow smile crept across Billy's damp face, as if in response to pleasant memories of times long past. The tired eyes opened, somewhat brighter now. "Ah, mate, she was a right good Mum, she was. Used to fix me soup, or broth, or maybe a little rabbit stew or somethin!" His smile widened at the thought. "Worked ever' time, too, it did! Always got me to feelin' better, right off." Another deep sigh escaped before he concluded weakly, "But she ain't here, she ain't, an' times is surely different…." His weary voice trailed off.

"Hey, I'll bet I can fix something like that for you, Billy! May not taste like your Mum's, but let's give it a try. You just stay quiet 'til I get back. We'll have you well again in no time!"

In spite of the danger of another confrontation with disgruntled natives, Geoffry slipped stealthily out of the fort and into the nearby woods. It was worth taking a chance, he told himself, if there was *anything* he could do to aid Billy's recovery. Still, deep inside, a secret fear gnawed at him ~ fear that what ailed his little companion was far more serious than just a simple fever or illness. He cringed to think that what Billy had contracted might well be one more manifestation of the dread malady that had already taken so many *other* lives in the settlement: *malaria*.

Cautiously Geoffry moved among the trees, wary, alert, stopping frequently to listen and observe his surroundings. Step by step, he penetrated deeper into the shadows until he was brought to an abrupt halt: a strangled squeal echoed just ahead, fracturing the deep hush of the forest. Geoffry ducked for cover behind a thick pile of underbrush. The noise had not sounded like a human cry, but its unnerving *nearness* made him aware of the need for utmost vigilance.

Hearing nothing further, Geoffry carefully parted the bushes and peered from his hiding place. In a small clearing just ahead he saw the source of the commotion: a young red fox, evidently in search of its dinner, had succeeded in surprising a squirrel and was about to savor the results of its hunting prowess.

Geoffry saw his opportunity. Without an effective weapon, he knew he had no chance of bringing down any game himself, either large or small. But here a fox had done the job *for* him ~ *if* he could persuade the predator to part with its prize!

Grasping a piece of limb for a club, Geoffry crashed through the brush toward the fox, emitting a shrill screech in an attempt to intimidate the crafty hunter. If he could just *frighten* the fox enough to keep it from carrying off its prey.....

His ploy succeeded! The startled fox, evidently fearing more for its life than for its stomach, bounded off with a yelp, leaving its anticipated meal behind.

When Geoffry returned to the cabin with his booty, he found Billy had fallen into a restless sleep ~ bed covers tangled about him, his brow beaded with perspiration. As quietly as possible, Geoffry skinned and dressed out the small carcass and dropped it into a pot of water. Next he hung the pot over the coals in their recently completed new stone fireplace.

Stirring up the fire and adding more wood to speed the cooking process, Geoffry noted with a touch of pride that it was not long before the water began to boil. Soon the steaming contents of the pot filled the shelter with a savory, appetizing aroma. To the mixture he next added a few greens, some of the tuberous roots he had found, a dried bay leaf, and just a tiny pinch of salt from their nearly exhausted store. Then he waited for Billy to waken.

The wait was not long. Evidently detecting the aromatic new scent even as he slept, Billy jerked awake, eyes blinking. Slowly he raised himself on one elbow and stared around. As Geoffry hurried to Billy's bedside, he was greeted with a mumbled, "Hey mate, I was just havin' me a great ol' dream, I was! My Mum was fixin' me some rabbit stew, she was, just like she used to, an' tellin' me everthin' was gonna be alright, an' all. And the stew smelled just like…just like…." He paused, as though confused at what his senses were detecting, his eyes still searching the small room. "And it smelled azzackly like what I'm smellin' *right now*, it did! What ya got cookin' in there, anyway, mate?" He gestured toward the boiling pot.

"I really *am* making you some stew, Billy, just like in your dream! Won't taste as good as your Mum's, I'm sure, but I hope its good enough to get you feeling better."

A wan smile softened the flushed face. "You do beat all, mate, ya surely do! Wherever did ya get meat an' all to make a *stew*, anyway? Have ya learned black magic or somethin'?"

Geoffry laughed. "No, Billy, it's just plain old squirrel." He explained how he had acquired the prized morsel.

"I done said it before, mate, but I'll say it again: you do beat all! Yesiree, you're a good mate, ya are!" Then he posed the most pressing question: "Do ya s'pose it's ready to eat yet?"

With another laugh, Geoffry got Billy's wooden bowl, ladled some of the steaming stew into it, then took it over to his companion. "Careful, Billy, it's pretty hot. Now, let's see if this'll cure what's wrong with you!"

He watched with happy satisfaction as Billy devoured the stew with obvious relish, pausing only to scrape the bowl and lick his spoon, then murmer, "Tastes just almost azzackly like what my Mum made, it does. Yesiree! You're a good mate, ya are!"

Pleased with the high praise, Geoffry grinned as he asked, "Can I get you some more, Billy? Or some water or anything?"

Billy sank back on his bed. "Nah, mate, that'll do 'er, it will. But that was right good, it was, an' no mistake!" A contented sigh escaped him. "Think I'll get me just a little more rest now. But thank ya kindly, Geoffry! You truly are a good mate!"

Before Geoffry could respond, Billy had again drifted off to sleep. Geoffry laid his hand on the damp brow and knew at once that the fever was not abating. His deepest fears for his little comrade returned. If Billy had actually come down with malaria, Geoffry knew only too well that there was scant chance for improvement or recovery. All he could do was make his friend as comfortable as possible, then wait and hope.

As Billy slept fitfully, tossing and turning, several times he muttered a faint, "Mum! Mum!" When next he awoke a few hours later, the fever appeared to have worsened rather than waned. "Could I have just a little more water, please?" he mumbled. After a few sips, he signaled for Geoffry to lean closer, a mixture of pain and pleading reflecting in his reddened eyes: "Now, can I ask ya a mighty big favor, mate, maybe my lastest one?"

"Of course you can, Billy, anything at all! Only please don't talk like it might be your final request! Please, Billy! You've just *got* to get better! You're the only mate I've got!"

A smile flickered across the moistened face at Geoffry's words. "This here's the favor, mate," Billy began, his voice weak and tremulous, interrupted by an occasional cough. "I guess ya knows by now that I never learned how to read or write none, I didn't. So's here's what I'm askin': I'd like ya to write a letter for me, I would, a letter to my Mum. I'd like ya to tell her what we been doin' since we come over here, an' all. And tell her how I'm always thinkin' 'bout her. And tell her I'm sorry I didn't git rich so's I could make her life all fine.... But I love her a whole lot, I do, and I 'preciate all what she done for me all them years." Another coughing spell interrupted. "Promise you'll do that for me, will ya, mate? Will ya *promise?*"

Geoffry dropped to his knees beside the bed and clutched his little friend in an affectionate embrace. "Billy, Billy, I *truly promise* I'll write your letter, and I'll see that your Mum gets it, too, no matter what! But please don't talk anymore like everything's over and you're not going to get better! Please, Billy!" He could no longer hold back the tears.

Billy's face lit briefly in a faint smile. "Like I been sayin, you're a right good mate, ya are," he murmured, then sank back on the bed. Soon his labored breathing indicated that he was once more deep in sleep.

Anxiously Geoffry waited at the bedside, watching, listening, feeling totally helpless. As the hours dragged by he dozed off on occasion, only to waken with a start to check again on the condition of his slumbering partner. He was relieved, almost reassured to find that, hour after hour, the sturdy little man still clung tenaciously to life.

Chapter 19

Through the long night, Geoffry kept his watchful vigil. Even when he felt his eyelids begin to sag with weariness, the slightest movement, the smallest sound from Billy's bed brought him back to complete wakefulness.

With the first streaks of morning light, Billy's unsettled sleep ended. He opened his tired eyes, jaded with fatigue and pain, and glanced warily about as though trying desperately to remember where he was. At last his gaze settled on Geoffry and his eyes brightened, a feeble smile slowly softening the drawn face. In a subdued voice he greeted his partner: "Mornin', mate. I take it ya slept well?"

"Good morning to you, Billy! Feeling any better today?" Geoffry reached to touch his friend's forehead. "Hey, I don't think your fever is as high today! You don't feel nearly as hot. That's great! I'll bet you really *are* getting better! Can I get you anything? Maybe some water?"

Again Billy tried to smile, without much success. "Thank you, mate, that's mighty kind o' ya, it is," he responded without enthusiasm. He managed to sip a bit of the water Geoffry brought him, then fell back on his bed. "Don't mean to be complainin' or nothin', mate, but my head feels like its about ready to esplode wide open this mornin,' it does. Maybe I need just a wee bit more sleep after all." The weary eyes closed slowly and Billy breathed heavily, exhausted by the exertion it took to speak.

A brief period of relative quiet ensued, but it was shattered abruptly by a loud, insistent banging on their door. "Hey Payne, ya in there? Open this here door, ya hear, an' right now!" It was the unmistakable, aggravating voice of Pike Perliss.

"*Now* what can that idiot want?" Geoffry muttered to himself as he strode to the door. Opening it, he found himself face to face with his old adversary. "What are *you* doing here, Perliss? What's all this fuss about?" he began, deeply annoyed by the intrusion. Then he noticed that Pike Perliss was not alone. Standing a few paces behind were two armed guards, men Geoffry recognized as being part of the small military cadre trained by Captain John Smith before his departure.

"Let's jist see if'n yer still sa smarty atter ya finds out why we's here, Payne," Pike chortled as he pushed his way past Geoffry into the cabin. Inside, he halted for a moment to examine once again the unique stone floor. Next, his meandering gaze settled on the new stone fireplace, and his eyes widened. Stomping across the room for a closer look, Pike ran a hand over the beautifully set stones. His self-satisfied, calculating smirk widened even further as he mumbled to himself, "Well, well, jist so much th' better...."

Finally glancing toward the bed where Billy lay with eyes closed, Pike demanded, "What's wrong wi' th' runt?"

"Billy isn't feeling well, so you leave him alone!" Geoffry felt his anger rising at Pike's over-bearing manner. "Now, I asked you before, Perliss: what're you *doing* here?"

"My, my, kinda testy this mornin,' ain't we though? Well, I reckons ya'll get over *that* soon a'nuff." Pike burst into a raucous laugh, then went on, "We is here on oh'fishal bizness, we is, Payne. You is ordered ta 'peer a'fore th' *Council*, ya is! Ya hear me? Yer ta come wif' us! An yer ta come *right now!*"

There was obvious relish in Pike's delivery of his ultimatum, and the presence of the armed guards underscored the seriousness of the matter. Still, it took Geoffry a few seconds to grasp that he was actually being summoned. "The *Council?*" he responded in disbelief. "What in Heaven's name could the Council want with *me*? At this hour? I've got to stay here and look after Billy!"

"Oh no ya don't, Payne! Yer comin' wif' us, like I said, an' yer comin' *now!* Or does ya wants we sh'ud jist shoot ya right here an' save ever'one a heap o' time an' trouble?" Pike erupted in another harsh, grating laugh. He signaled the two guards to secure Geoffry and compel him to comply with the order.

Seeing that resistance under the circumstances would be futile, Geoffry acquiesced. "Well then, let's hurry up and get it over with. I'd like to find out what this is all about so I can get back here as quick as possible!" As he went out the door, he called out, "Don't worry, Billy, I'll be back soon!" But he wasn't sure Billy was even awake or aware enough to realize what was taking place.

When the four men reached the guardhouse, Geoffry saw that the members of the Council of Virginia had already assembled. In spite of the fact that George Percy had been chosen officially to serve as President of the Council, it became clearly evident that *real* power had devolved once more upon Gabriel Archer. The barrister greeted Geoffry with a sneer. "Well, Payne, it's about *time* you got here, isn't it? You certainly took long enough! I say, your type doesn't seem to mind wasting the time of your betters, now do you?" Archer's chin jutted out and he sniffed his disdain.

A sarcastic reply flashed through Geoffry's mind, but he withheld it. "Perliss said you wanted to see me. What's this all about, anyway?"

"Silence! *We'll* ask the questions around here! Now, get inside and let's get on with the proceedings."

Geoffry was not intimidated. "Proceedings? *What* 'proceedings'? I've got nothing to say to you, Archer, or to any of your lackeys here! I need to get back to Billy!"

Archer drew himself up, glaring at Geoffry. "Enough of your insolence, Payne! I say, you still don't seem to know your place, do you? Have a care, or I'll have the guards clap you in irons right now! It's about time you learned to show proper respect for those in authority, by Jove!"

Realizing he could not accomplish anything by further antagonizing the arrogant Archer, Geoffry marched through the door of the guardhouse, head held high. The Council members took their places on make-shift seats, while Geoffry was prodded to his spot standing before the group.

President Percy cleared his throat and began: "It has been brought to our attention that you, Geoffry Payne, common laborer, were detected in the act of thievery. Do you understand, according to my decree, what the punishment *is* for thievery? What have you to say for yourself?"

Totally stunned by the absurdity of the charges, Geoffry could only stare at the Council in incredulity. He was dumbfounded! Yet as he surveyed the faces of the Council members, he realized that they were absolutely in earnest about the charges. He shook his head in complete disbelief!

"President Percy, if you please, that is the most ridiculous accusation I have ever heard! *Thievery? Me*? Exactly what is it that I'm supposed to have *stolen*, anyway?"

Gabriel Archer interrupted: "Same old Payne, aren't you? Just don't seem to understand how to appropriately address your superiors, do you now? Well, you'll learn soon enough, I daresay!"

Geoffry leveled a withering glance at Archer but did not reply. Instead, he turned his back as much as possible on the arrogant lawyer and repeated his question: "President Percy, can you please tell me what it is I'm accused of *stealing?*"

"Why, food, man, *food*, as if you didn't know! You were seen entering the storehouse without permission. And you know as well as anyone that the storehouse is now empty of all provisions. Do you dare to deny this?"

"Of *course* I know the storehouse is empty. It has been for a *weeks*, as you all know very well yourselves! So how could I possibly have *stolen* anything?"

"That's not the point, Payne," Archer interjected. "The point is, you were seen going where you had no right to be. You went into the storehouse. Now the supplies are gone. I say, it's as clear and simple as that."

The logic behind the charges was so convoluted, so bizarre, Geoffry found it difficult to believe any sane person could take them seriously. "And who supposedly *saw* me doing this dastardly deed?" he burst out, his hereditary temper near the breaking point.

"Not that it's any of your business, but you were observed by a most loyal and reliable member of our community ~ Mr. Pike Perliss! You should also be aware, Payne, that the so-called 'Captain' John Smith is no longer around to protect you, so have a care!"

"*Pike Perliss? That* lying snake? This has to be some kind of grotesque *joke!* Why, Perliss would murder his own grandmother if he thought he could profit from it! *'Loyal and reliable'? Ha!* Have you all gone *insane?*" Geoffry's frustration seethed as he surveyed the blank faces before him.

Perliss apparently saw Geoffry's outburst as an opportunity to further ingratiate himself with the Council. Stepping forward, he grasped Geoffry's arm roughly as he growled, "Have a care there, Payne, or ol' Pike'll hafta teach ya some manners, he will! Showin' no respeck fer these good gennelmens! But I reckons ya'll change yer tune quick enough, ya will, when *yer* hangeded an' *I* moves inta yer fancy house! Now whaddaya think o' *that?*"

Geoffry was flabbergasted. "So *that's* it, is it? *That's* what this is all about?" He turned to face the malevolent Gabriel Archer. "And I'll just bet *you're* the one behind it all, aren't you, Archer, you pompous ass! You bribed this devious fraud to *lie* about me, didn't you? You promised him that if he did he could have our *house* when I was dead! Well, well! So much for all of your righteous talk about 'superiority.' You're every bit as depraved as Perliss is, you slimy rat! And you're doing all this just to get back at Captain Smith somehow, aren't you? You're willing to destroy *anyone* who recognizes that the Captain is a man of true ability! Well, let me tell you this, Archer: in spite of all of your phony airs and fancy trappings, you're not fit to clean the Captain's *outhouse!*"

For a moment Gabriel Archer sat silent, ashen-faced, apparently stunned by the audacity of Geoffry's attack. Then he sprang from his seat, stark hatred burning in his eyes, and slapped Geoffry viciously across the mouth. Turning to his startled colleagues, Archer announced primly, "Well, I certainly don't see any need for further deliberations. You've all heard the charges, and you've witnessed the boorish, uncivilized behavior of the accused. Therefore I propose that we remand this felon to that cell over there, to be held until arrangements can be made for him to be *hanged* ~ which won't take *long!*" He finished with an ominous glare at Geoffry.

There was no discussion, no disagreement, no vote. Instead, President of the Council Percy merely nodded, adding in a muted voice, "Well then! It is so ordered!" With that, the Council filed out behind the pretentious Archer, a grinning Pike Perliss traipsing along behind.

Chapter 20

▼

"We hates to do this to ya, Payne, you bein' a friend o' Billy an' all," one of the guards apologized after the Council members had gone. "But orders is orders, so into the cell ya goes!"

At mention of Billy's name, Geoffry turned to look more closely at the man who had spoken. "Wait a minute, weren't you one of the guards here when they threw Captain Smith in jail? You're the one who was a shipmate of Billy's, aren't you?"

"Right ya are, Payne. Me an' Billy was shipmates, sure enough. An' we surely did have us some good ol' times together, we did! I understands *you're* his new mate now, ain't ya?"

"Yes, we met working on the docks, and we came over together on the 'Susan Constant.' Been friends ever since." Geoffry paused for a moment. "But I'm afraid Billy's not doing so well right now."

"Oh? What's the matter? He sick or somethin'?"

"Yes, he's *very* sick, with a real high fever and everything. I was afraid he might have come down with malaria. But he seemed a little better this morning, except for a terrible headache."

"Headache? Ya say he gots a headache now?"

"Yes, and it seemed to be a pretty bad one."

The guard looked down at the floor, shaking his head slowly. "I'm afeerd that don't sound so good, it don't," he muttered.

"Why? What do you mean?"

"Well, ya see, the mate what I had after we come over here, he got the malaria too, he did. Got all hot an' feverish, just like ya say Billy done. Then just when we thunk he was gettin' better, he woke up with this awful headache." He stopped, still obviously disturbed by the memory. "Next day, he was gone."

"You think that's what's going to happen to Billy? That it's a sign he's going to *die?*"

"Nah, I ain't sayin' Billy's gonna die, I ain't. It's just that...." His voice trailed off. After a moment, he straightened and concluded in a steadier voice, "Anyways, I gots ta put ya in that there jail now, I does." He unlocked the cell and escorted Geoffry inside, then carefully closed and re-locked the door.

Before the guard could leave, Geoffry called out a request: "One more thing: Do you suppose you could look in on Billy for me sometime soon? He was sleeping when you took me away, but he's going to need someone to keep an eye on him, and...," he glanced around the cell, "and it doesn't look like I'll be able to do very much for him from in here."

"Yeah, be happy to. Be good to see ol' Billy again, it will! I'll traipse on over by your place on m' way back."

After expressing his sincere appreciation to the guard, Geoffry settled down on the bare boards of the bunk that was his cell's only furnishing, pondering the morning's events. It all still seemed so preposterous, so absurd it was hard to fathom! Yet here he was, facing a future that looked anything but promising, to say the least. Worst of all, it was keeping him from fulfilling what he felt was his *highest* priority and responsibility: taking care of his friend Billy.

Hour after hour dragged by with no word from guards or Council, no food or water, no interruptions of any kind to his solitary confinement. The onset of evening darkness only added to the gloom of both his cell and his spirits. Geoffry knew only too well that Gabriel Archer would be true to his word and make all haste to carry out the imposed death sentence. He tried to suppress rising feelings of foreboding, but with little success. And when he did finally doze off, he was jolted awake by a haunting nightmare ~ a nightmare that came in the shape of a gallows.

Fully awake as a result of his ominous dream, Geoffry was brought sharply to attention. He thought he heard a surreptitious, almost inaudible sound coming from outside the guardhouse, like the shuffle of stealthy footsteps! He swung his feet over the side of the low bunk, sat up, and listened even more intently. It came again: an almost imperceptible crunch, now just beyond the door. Next, a furtive scraping and a metallic click told Geoffry that someone was actually unlocking the guardhouse door! Who could it be, he wondered? The room was enshrouded in darkness, meaning that morning was still hours away.

He remained motionless, almost afraid to breathe, as he heard the door open slowly, very slowly ~ as though someone were trying to minimize any protesting squeak from the rusty hinges. It closed again softly, still with no indication as to who might have entered the room. More muffled footsteps sounded, this time moving directly toward his cell. Then a low, weak voice whispered, "Hey mate! Are ya in there?"

Geoffry sprang from his bunk, his mind alternating wildly between absolute disbelief and fleeting hope as he recognized the familiar accent. "Billy! Is that *you* out there? What on earth are you doing here? In the middle of the night? Why aren't you back home in bed, where you belong? And how were you able to get in here, anyway?"

"Whoa, now! Slow down just a minute, will ya mate?" Billy's voice was weak, barely audible, but he managed a low chuckle at Geoffry's bewildered curiosity.

"But Billy, you're the last person in the whole wide *world* I'd expect to see here! Are you feeling better now? You can't be strong enough yet to have come this far!"

"Tell the truth, mate, I used up 'bout every bit o' strength what I had left gettin' here, I did! Mind if I sits here on one o' these crates and rests a spell?" There was a pause while Billy found a place to sit. Next he rattled something mysteriously in the darkness. "And do ya know what I brung, mate? These here is *keys*, they is. I come to get ya out o' that there cell, I did, an' right quick!"

"You say you've got *keys*, Billy? How in the world....? Hey, you just stay sitting right where you are for a while! You just *shouldn't* have come all this way, as sick as you are! But I'll tell you, you're a mighty welcome sight, no mistake!" Geoffry stopped for a moment, then added, "And I'd really like to know how you managed to get *hold* of the keys to this guardhouse, Billy. You're something else, you truly are! Now, why don't you toss those keys over this way and I'll see if I can find one that'll open this cell."

"Oh, it's on the ring somewheres, alright. I knows it is." Billy's toss was a bit short, but Geoffry managed to reach through the bars and grope in the darkness until he retrieved the keys. After a few moments of fumbling, he located the proper one and unlocked the cell door. With a bound, he reached Billy and wrapped the little man in an encompassing bear hug.

"It's really, really good to see you, Billy! Everything happened so fast this morning I wasn't sure if you even knew what was going on. I know *I* didn't! Now, as soon as you've had a chance to catch your breath, you've just *got* to explain how you knew to come find me! And how you ended up with those jail keys! Like I said, you're something else again!"

The pleased look on Billy's face in the faint light said far more than the words he seemed to find difficult to utter. Then, appearing to muster all of his remaining strength, he explained in a faltering voice: "It was like this, mate: My ol' shipmate come to see me, he did, like he said ya axed him to. He told me what happened to ya, an' all. And he brung along a bottle o' wine what he said that snake Archer had give 'im. Now where Archer got wine when everyone else here is starvin,' Lord only knows! Anyway, he give the wine to my shipmate for doin' his duty 'above and beyond,' whatever *that* means. My friend wanted to share with me, but I was feelin' pretty poorly, I was, so's he ended up drinkin' the whole bottle hisself. Well, pretty soon he began to get real sleepy-like. Then he started in snorin,' makin' practical enough racket to crack our new floor! So's I snuck over an' snitched his keys, I did. Far as I knows, he's *still* snorin' back there! Then I come here as quick as I could to get ya outta this jail, I did. Yesiree! Can't let my mate get hunged, now can I?" He halted his labored recitation in a fit of coughing.

"Billy, Billy, I swear, I don't know *how* you managed to do all that! You're still so very sick, and now you look just completely tuckered out! Would you like me to help you back to our cabin before I go? I don't think I'd better stick around here very long, what with Archer threatening to hang me as soon as it's daylight. And I'm just sure the whole reason he's doing all this is because we were friends with Captain Smith! But he's dead serious about it, anyway!"

"Nah, mate, don't you worry none 'bout me. I'll be fine right here, I will. I'll just rest me some on your bunk in there. But be sure to lock the doors when ya leave, and then why don't ya throw them keys away somewheres? That way it'll take 'em a lot longer to find out ya ain't in here no more! Me oh my! It'll be somethin' else to see ol' Archer's face when he finds *me* in here 'stead o' you, won't it now?" Billy couldn't repress a feeble chuckle.

"Well, if you're *sure* you'll be all right, I guess I *should* get going, and fast!" Geoffry hesitated. "What I'd *really* like is to be able to stay here and look after you, Billy! But I guess I couldn't do very much for you if I'm hanged, could I?" He paused again, then concluded in a voice choked with heart-felt emotion, "I sure do hate to leave you, though, Billy! You've been such a great mate!"

Geoffry helped his partner into the vacated cell and onto the bunk, then stopped once more to clutch him in a warm embrace. He patted the ailing, unsteady little man's shoulder, whispering softly, "Goodbye, Billy. Thank you for saving my life!"

"Bye, mate. I reckon maybe that kinda makes us *even* now, don't it? Anyway, ya best get movin,' an' mighty *quick*, 'fore someone comes along."

Locking both the cell door and guardhouse door behind him, Geoffry eased silently into the pre-dawn darkness. He had no weapons, no food, no supplies, only the knowledge that to remain where he was meant certain death. With a hasty backward glance at the place that had been his home for the past two years, he slipped through the gates of James Fort and headed for the relative security of the surrounding forest.

Meanwhile, back in the cell that Geoffry had so recently vacated, Billy sank back on the rough boards of the bunk, his breath coming in labored gasps. He tried to imagine the direction of Geoffry's flight, or what his plans might be. But he found himself confused, overwhelmed by complete listlessness, by absolute exhaustion of both mind and body. Slowly, bit by bit, he felt himself relax. As his weariness faded, Billy Bascomb slipped silently, serenely into an uncharted realm of peace and perfect tranquility.

Chapter 21

▼

Wary, cautious, alert for any sound or movement, Geoffry hurried along the narrow woodland path that paralleled the James River. Deep within, he knew he really had no alternative to the course of action he was taking. Still, he could not escape his sense of acute personal regret: regret that he had been compelled to abandon Billy at a truly critical time, and regret at being forced to leave the little settlement he had worked so hard to help establish ~ this first English "foothold" in a strange new land.

In addition to regret, there remained also lingering resentment at the arbitrary *power* wielded by James' Towne's small elite ruling group. Though totally unproductive in the colony's day-to-day operations, as Geoffry knew only too well from his experiences, these individuals nevertheless insisted on receiving all of the benefits accruing from the labor of the majority. It was a flawed system, in his thinking, and he felt intensely that the system needed correction. Yet, he realized also that entrenched groups like the Council of Virginia did not yield power easily. Perhaps it would ultimately take *revolutionary* action to effect change, Geoffry reflected. But he felt certain that in time, one way or another, the diversified environment of this New World *would* engender change.

Along with these thoughts, *another* factor filtered gradually into Geoffry's consciousness ~ a momentous perception that brought with it a truly gratifying thrill! Since he had been forced to flee James' Towne totally against his own will and only to save his life, Geoffry realized, he could now no longer be held liable to fulfill his *indenture* obligation to the London Company! It certainly would be difficult to work off his debt if he were *hanged*, he told himself wryly. And he had, after all, been driven out by actions of the Company's own governing Council. It left him with no possible *means* of providing labor in exchange for the price of his passage to Virginia. *He was free!*

Despite the latent euphoria, however, there still remained a most immediate and pressing need: to put as much distance between himself and James' Towne as possible, and as rapidly as possible! Knowing how deeply and stubbornly the resentful Gabriel Archer held a grudge, Geoffry was certain he would not be permitted to escape easily from the lawyer's relentless wrath. To defy Archer and get away with it would set an unacceptable precedent! Therefore Geoffry expected to be pursued tenaciously, and he could expect absolutely no mercy should he be apprehended and returned to face his imposed judgement, no matter how contrived or unjust the sentence might have been.

Accordingly, he moved through the forest as swiftly as he dared, utilizing the trail when he felt it safe but retreating deeper into the timberland whenever the path led through open meadows. Further, he had decided not to try to make his escape by heading north or west from the settlement, areas that were at least partially familiar to him because of his explorations with Captain Smith. He was sure that this is exactly what Archer would expect. Instead, Geoffry followed the north bank of the James River *eastward* in the general direction of Chesapeake Bay, hoping eventually to find a place where he could cross the river and turn south. Precisely where he was headed Geoffry had no idea whatsoever. What he *did* know was that he needed to get as far from both James' Towne and Gabriel Archer as possible!

As he maintained his constant but vigilant pace, Geoffry became more and more conscious of growing hunger and fatigue. Having had nothing to eat since the previous morning, and with only brief intervals of fitful sleep throughout the night, he felt his energy steadily waning. Still, to stop for rest now, he knew, would only add to the danger that some pursuer might catch up with him. It would be best to press on.

As the day wore on, however, Geoffry found it impossible to resist an occasional pause as he passed a bush laden with ripe wild berries, or to take a few sips of water from the seaward-flowing James. And by mid-afternoon, now miles from James' Towne with all of its dangers, he felt safe enough to look for a place to hide, some sort of concealment, where perhaps he could get a little sleep. Leaving the trail to push through the heavy underbrush alongside, he came upon a jumbled patch of blackberry vines cascading in profusion over and around the trunk of a huge long-fallen cedar tree. By forcing his way carefully along the trunk, he was able to penetrate under the brambles far enough to create a small hideaway, a spot he felt would serve as a secure sleeping site. He pulled some of the brambles back across the opening he had made, then snuggled down into a bed of needles and leaves next to the trunk. Within minutes, in spite of all his anxieties and concerns, he was fast asleep.

How long he had slept Geoffry had no idea. All he knew was that he was awakened abruptly, unceremoniously by the rasping tones of a brusque, obnoxious, familiar voice: "Hey Payne, I know's ya's in there! Now git on out here, ya hear me, a'fore I blasts ya!" Unmistakably, it was Pike Perliss! Once again, it appeared, Geoffry was about to be confronted by his dogged nemesis.

Geoffry's sleep-clogged brain was slow to grasp what was happening. He lay completely still, trying to gather his thoughts, trying to decide what he should do, trying to fathom how Pike Perliss could possibly have found him. But he was given little time for reflection. The ominous threat was repeated, even louder this time: "Ya heered me, Payne! I ain't a'foolin'! Git out here, an' right now, or ol' Pike'll jist hafta shoot ya dead an' then drag yer puny body back ta th' fort, he will!" Pike's grating laugh echoed through the woodland, rendering the entire situation even more bizzare.

Still unsure whether Pike could actually see him in his covert hiding place or was merely bluffing, Geoffry hesitated a moment longer. All doubt was removed, however, when the din of a musket blast shattered the sylvan stillness and a lead ball ripped through the brambles mere inches from Geoffry's head. It was accompanied by a snarling, "I tol' ya ta come *out*, Payne! An I means *now!*"

"All right, Perliss, hold your fire! I'm coming out!" Geoffry shouted, finding no alternative to surrender.

Gingerly he worked his way back out of the maze of blackberry brambles. And there waiting for him stood Pike Perliss, grinning from ear to ear, his musket at the ready in case Geoffry should entertain any notion of trying to escape by making a sudden dash into the woods.

"So ya thought ya could fool ol' Pike, didja' Payne, an git away fr'm th' Council?" Perliss emitted another triumphant cackle. "Well, jist look at who's havin' th' last laugh! Yer goin back ta be th' star at yer very own hangin', ya is!" Perliss couldn't resist another raucous guffaw at his witticism. "Anyways, I gots ta git ya back ta th' fort an' git ya proper hangded, I does, like Mr. Archer wants. Otherwise I doesn't git ta have yer house, remem'er? So you come along, an' *right now!*"

"Oh, I wouldn't *think* of depriving you of your rightful property, Perliss, so I'll be only too happy to accompany you!" Geoffry's sarcasm was completely lost on Pike, who could only smirk at Geoffry's apparent cooperation. "But can I ask you a question first: just how did you manage to trace me and find me, hidden away like I was?"

"Aw, that there's th' bes' part, it is, Payne. Ya see, ever' one else were jist sure ya was gonna head upriver, they was, like ya done wi' that mangy Cap'n Smith. But not ol' Pike! Nosiree! He weren't fooled one bit! I jist figgered ya'd do the azzact *opposite*, I did, you bein' sa contrary an' all. So's I follered th' trail *downstream*, instead. An' guess what I seed? It were boot prints, made by reg'lar English boots, it was, mixed right in wi' all them moccasin tracks. Yesiree! Ol' Pike knowed right off what way ya was headed, he did! Jist follered them there boot prints 'til finally they took off inta th' woods. Weren't hard ta guess where ya was a' hidin', neither, cuz it's azzackly th' kinda' hidin' place I'da prob'ly been lookin' fer m'self! An' sure anuff, there ya was!" Relating the tale of his deductive prowess brought on another burst of unrestrained merriment.

"Well, I have to hand it to you, Perliss, I really do! I am surprised! I just never would have thought you were *smart* enough to figure out what I was up to, to tell the truth."

"Heyyy, you watch yer mouf, Payne! It ain't too late ta shoot ya yet, ya knows, 'ceptin I don't wanna hafta drag yer stinkin' corpse all that way back! So you jist shut yer mouf an' git a'movin', ya hear?"

As the two got set to begin their trek back toward James' Towne, Pike's self-aggrandizing machinations underwent a sudden and dramatic shift in course. Without so much as the snap of a twig to provide a warning, half a dozen warriors attired in full fighting regalia materialized noiselessly from the woods and encircled the two startled white men. The sound of Pike's musket shot had evidently drawn their attention. With menacing signals and gestures, they now advanced toward the pair step by step, closing the surrounding ring ever tighter.

Geoffry and Pike both looked warily from side to side, from warrior to warrior, but there was no avenue of escape. In desperation, Pike raised his musket to his shoulder and aimed at the nearest native, bellowing in rage, "I'll fix ya, I will, ya bloody heathen!" But just as he squeezed the trigger, another warrior lunged forward with a heart-stopping shriek, delivering a crushing, disabling blow to Pike's arm with his tomahawk. The musket ball sailed harmlessly off through the woods.

Screeching in pain as blood spurted from his mutilated arm, Pike dropped his weapon and turned to run. But once more all flight was cut off. Several of the nearest warriors now leaped to grapple with the disabled Pike and pin him roughly against a tree. Another produced buckskin thongs, and with these Pike was quickly rendered helpless ~ his arms pulled backward around the trunk of the tree, where his wrists were lashed firmly together.

As Pike continued his screaming and cursing, the warriors turned to Geoffry, pinioning him to another tree in similar fashion. Then, forming a circle around the two men, the natives began a dance of death, brandishing their weapons in menacing fashion, halting occasionally to spit on their prisoners or to jab them with the tips of their spears. Geoffry scarcely dared to breathe, remaining completely silent despite the pain, waiting for the end he was certain would come momentarily. Pike Perliss, by contrast, increased the volume of his howls and curses with each new jab.

As the ritual neared a frenzied crescendo, one of the warriors suddenly stopped, raising a hand to signal the others to halt as well. Pointing toward a lone figure approaching along the forest trail, he uttered a single word ~ unintelligible to Geoffry but evidently one that symbolized the power and authority represented by the newcomer. Immediately the natives stopped, facing in the direction from which the individual was advancing. Next they dropped to one knee and lowered their heads. Even Pike Perliss quieted for a moment, less in deference it seemed than out of curiosity.

The visitor strode into the midst of the group and exchanged greetings. His beautifully ornamented buckskin clothing, his erect posture, the arrangement of his elaborate feathered headpiece all indicated a personage of high standing, someone to be respected. And yet, as Geoffry observed the proceedings, a feeling grew that there was something distinctly familiar about this newcomer.

As the warriors rose to their feet, the visitor turned to view the two prisoners. At sight of Geoffry, his eyes widened in surprise, and a broad smile of recognition spread across his face. Stepping closer to look directly at Geoffry, he said, "You Geoffry Payne!"

"*Wawoka!*" Geoffry could scarcely believe it was possible! First he had been rescued by Billy. Now, at an equally critical juncture, a *second* sympathetic compatriot had miraculously appeared!

Wawoka turned to announce to the others: "Wawoka, Geoffry Payne *friends!* He Wawoka's *friend!*"

Excited murmurs broke from the warriors as they gathered around Geoffry. There was a momentary uneasiness, since they were not sure how Wawoka would respond to the capture of his comrade and their marking him for death. But Wawoka's pleasure at being reunited with his old friend quickly allayed all fears. At a signal, Geoffry was cut loose and the two men engaged in a hearty embrace.

"I really, really am glad to see you again, Wawoka," Geoffry proclaimed, patting the Indian affectionately on the back. "And not just because you saved my life, either!"

Wawoka appeared perplexed for a moment, then nodded vigorously in comprehension. "Geoffry Payne save Wawoka's life, Wawoka save Geoffry's life! We *friends!*"

Geoffry erupted in laughter, both in relief and with true delight. "We friends!" he repeated, and Wawoka joined in his merriment.

At last Wawoka turned to view the second prisoner, still tied securely to his tree. Recognition once again brought stunned surprise. But this time a dark shadow of unmitigated contempt swept across Wawoka's face, while from his dark eyes flashed pure hatred and anger. Wawoka strode to within mere inches of Pike's face and spat out, "You Pike Perliss!"

"Yeah, it's ol' Pike, awright, ain't it now?" Pike's tone was fawning, his manner groveling. "It's good ol' Pike hisself!" Then, attempting to mimic the exact tone Wawoka had used with Geoffry, he added, "Pike Perliss Wawoka's *friend!*"

"*No!*" Wawoka exploded. "Pike Perliss _not_ Wawoka's friend! Pike Perliss *evil man!*"

To help the assembled war party understand, Wawoka lifted his beaded buckskin shirt, revealing the crisscross of scars still visible on his body. "Perliss cut Wawoka with knife! And Perliss _shoot_ Wawoka's young brother! Perliss *bad man!*"

Gasps of horror and unrestrainable anger seethed from the warriors at sight of Pike Perliss's grisly handiwork. With eyes blazing, several of those nearest sprang at the bound man and ripped off his shirt. Next they began systematically slashing Perliss's chest, carving the same crisscross patterns that he had inflicted upon Wawoka. Pike's shrieks of rage and agony, along with his vehement curses, seemed only to heighten their pleasure as they exacted their revenge.

In spite of the long train of abuses, the lies, the thievery, the duplicity and chicanery of which Pike Perliss had been guilty, Geoffry was still taken aback at the ferocity, the vicious cruelty of what he was now witnessing. It was too much, even for a person like Perliss! "Please, Wawoka, can't you stop them?" he pleaded. "I know Perliss is a very bad man, but even *he* doesn't deserve to die like this!"

Wawoka nodded. Drawing in a long breath, he stepped before the cringing, screaming Pike and looked deep into his bulging, fear-filled eyes. Then calmly Wawoka reached up and slashed Perliss's throat.

Chapter 22

"Goodbye, Wawoka. You've truly been a great friend! I hope we meet again somewhere in the future." Geoffry gripped the Indian leader's forearm, then gave him an amiable pat on the back before stepping into the waiting birchbark canoe. He had asked Wawoka for one last favor: to help him get safely across the James River so that he could renew his exodus from the grave dangers awaiting at James' Towne.

"Goodbye, Geoffry Payne," Wawoka responded as the little craft pushed off into the river's slack current. Wawoka raised his left hand, palm forward, and Geoffry waved back as the canoe cut swiftly across the water.

It had been a most wrenching, disturbing day, Geoffry reflected, one filled with hidden dangers and uncertainties, all ending finally with the brutal death of Pike Perliss. The war party had left Pike's mutilated body bound to the tree, apparently as a warning to other white settlers. Relations between the two cultures were destined to continue on a downhill slide, Geoffry was sure, as long as hostility and retaliation remained the accepted norms.

Geoffry had communicated to Wawoka his intention to travel south, as far from the settlement as possible, and he had then prevailed upon the Indian leader for assistance in crossing the James. Wawoka and his warriors had led Geoffry to a spot not far downstream where several canoes were concealed in a small well-protected cove. Evidently the craft were kept out of sight but readily available for use by anyone who had need of them, whether for hunting, fishing, or for any unforeseen emergency.

It was Geoffry's first venture in one of the fragile-looking craft, and he studied its structure with keen interest as it glided smoothly across the water, propelled by the paddles of two braves assigned to assist him. The framework was made of strips of cedar wood, carved or bent into the desired shapes, then lashed together with buckskin thongs. Around this skeleton a shell of birch bark "panels" had been attached, laced to the cedar framework with what looked like long flexible roots. The seams were sealed with pitch to render the canoe completely watertight. At each end, distinctive stitching had been utilized to fasten the pieces of bark securely where they met, and additional decorative designs gave the canoe an artistic as well as functional look. Altogether it was a sturdy, serviceable little craft despite its frail appearance ~ light in weight for easy portage when necessary, but capable of remarkable speed under the efforts of two paddle-wielding occupants.

When Geoffry turned for a last look at the receding shoreline, he saw Wawoka still watching their departure. Geoffry waved a final farewell and was pleased to see his friend respond. I'll probably never see him again, Geoffry thought to himself, and that's too bad. Just think what the outcome might be if we had a few more like him to *improve* relations between our two peoples! What a waste to always emphasize our *differences,* and so fuel distrust and enmity instead!

When the canoe reached the far shore of the James, the two warriors held it steady while Geoffry stepped out. "Thank you both for your help," he said as he shook their hands in turn. He wasn't sure if they actually understood what he was saying, but their response to his warm smile and respectful demeanor was clear.

"Goodbye, Wawoka's friend," one of them ventured as they pushed off for their return trip. "Goodbye, Geoffry Payne," added the other. Both men returned Geoffry's parting wave as they pulled away.

As the canoe navigated its way back across the James, diminishing into a tiny miniature by the time it reached the opposite shore, Geoffry continued to watch. He felt a vague reluctance to actually begin his trek farther toward the south, toward the unknown future that lay in that direction. For just a moment, a wave of foreboding swept over him. He realized that he had not been this alone since he left England! Now he was totally on his own, dependent only upon himself, with no one to turn to should he require assistance.

Second thoughts about his decision began to intrude. After all, he acknowledged with a surge of guilt, he had left Billy in what was truly an untenable position ~ dying, and in a jail cell. Had it been purely a self-serving decision? Had he abandoned his best friend at a critical time just to save his own life? He shuddered to think himself *capable* of such callousness! And furthermore, had he perhaps been *too hasty* in cutting off total contact with the James' Towne settlement? After all, some very good people still remained there, in spite of the hardships and starvation they had experienced and despite the lack of leadership exhibited by the Council.

But it took only a moment's reflection to recognize that there actually could have been no other *choice!* Had he stayed, death by hanging would have been his inevitable fate, as decreed by Archer and his cohorts. How could he have helped Billy *then?* At least here, though now alone in a vast forest, Geoffry felt he'd been given a *chance*, no matter how slim the odds that a stone-worker from Salisbury with limited frontier skills and knowledge could survive for long in a primeval wilderness.

When Geoffry had indicated that he planned to head south, Wawoka had been able to offer only vague advice: "Look for Croatoans, or Lumbee tribe." But he had not explained *why* Geoffry should seek out these two groups in particular, or where they were located. Now Geoffry could only wonder at the stark improbability of finding *either* of the tribes in the vast woodlands that stretched endlessly before him as far as the eye could see.

He took a deep breath, then gathered up the few possessions Wawoka had insisted he accept and prepared to set out. There wasn't much: a hunting knife, most likely obtained from some settler through trade; a tomahawk, its flint edge flaked to create a sharp, formidable weapon; a light blanket of buckskin; and for food, some dried strips of venison, or "pemmican" as the natives called it. It was the sum total of his worldly possessions! With a rueful smile, Geoffry thought how *different* this all was from the high expectations he had entertained when he originally reached the shores of Virginia. After all, he had been promised the first large nugget of *gold* as his reward for sighting the new land, he remembered, and almost laughed out loud. There had been such grand hopes ~ hopes of great riches and glory for *everyone!*

Yet, as he started down the narrow forest trail that led toward his new life, he knew he had not lost faith in what to him still constituted the *true* wealth of this New World: the endless acres of fertile *land*, stretching away to far distant horizons! With a bit of good luck and lots of hard work, Geoffry was certain that attaining his dream was *still* within the realm of possibility.

The late afternoon sun had almost disappeared in the western sky by now, and Geoffry knew he had to decide soon where to spend the night. Fortunately, what he had learned while on the expedition with Captain Smith made the process a bit easier, though it still required care and planning. The path he had been following appeared to be a trail used mostly by deer, judging from the profusion of hoof prints, and therefore Geoffry was sure it would eventually lead to fresh water. His hunch proved correct. Before long, he came to an open, swampy region with pools of water apparently fed by springs dotting the landscape in random fashion. The trail skirted the western edge of this marshy, bog-like area, but first Geoffry found one rather deep pool with water that looked reasonably clear. He dipped some out with his hand and took a few tentative sips. It had a faint bitter aftertaste but was nonetheless refreshing, and he couldn't resist some deeper draughts.

Then he made his way off the trail into the surrounding woods, and once again he found a patch of blackberry brambles, not too different from the one under which he had been hiding when Pike Perliss found him. Smiling wryly at the irony, Geoffry decided that this would still make a good sleeping spot, since Pike was no longer around to pose a threat. After picking several handfuls of berries to complement a strip of his pemmican, he enjoyed his light repast, then pushed his way through a small opening under the prickly vines. He patted down the leaves and humus and wrapped his buckskin blanket around himself. Before he'd had time to review all of the improbable events that had comprised this eventful day, he sank into a deep, exhausted sleep.

The cheerful chirping of woodland birds awakened him many hours later. For a time he just lay still, listening to the sounds of the forest, before reluctantly abandoning his sleeping place. After washing up at one of the pools and chewing another strip of his limited rations, he rolled his few possessions into a neat bundle, swung the pack onto his back, and set out once more.

This day's travel was much like that of the previous afternoon. The narrow animal trail continued to provide relatively easy passage through the timberland, and Geoffry kept following it since it led in the general direction he wished to go. Ever on the alert, not sure what to expect from either natives or nature, he was able to make steady progress, stopping only for an occasional drink of water or for anything that might serve as food.

It was the increasing scarcity of the latter commodity that gnawed at Geoffry's consciousness as he pushed on in his journey southward. The strips of dried meat would not last much longer, he knew, but he saw no immediate prospects for acquiring anything other than what the forest had to offer. He could feel the lack of nourishment beginning to affect his level of energy as he plodded on mile after mile.

When he finally halted for the night, he determined to try something he knew might well prove futile but would at least constitute an *effort* to obtain additional food. With the knife Wawoka had given him, he carefully cut long, thin strips of buckskin from the edge of his blanket. He tied these pieces securely end to end to create a length of thong, flexible and quite strong. Next, from his observations of the techniques used by Billy Bascomb, he fashioned a snare from the thong and set it out amidst the brush and saplings just off the trail. It wasn't much, he realized, but he had to try! Then, weary from the demands of the day, he wrapped himself in the remains of his blanket, snuggled down into a bed of leaves and cedar boughs, and quickly dropped off to sleep.

Restless both from fatigue and persistent anxiety, Geoffry was awakened by an intrusive low, rustling sound. It was still quite dark, though he could sense the first light of dawn not far off. Rising and moving noiselessly toward the commotion, his heartbeat quickened when he realized it was coming from the area where he had set his snare. Sure enough, as he peered through the brush, he saw a frightened hare thrashing wildly about, trying desperately to free itself from the makeshift snare. Despite his personal misgivings about the concept of "the law of the jungle," Geoffry knew that his very *survival* now hinged upon its exercise, and he dispatched his little victim as mercifully as possible.

After dressing out the carcass, Geoffry decided to risk a small fire to prepare his catch for breakfast. A serious realization quickly dawned upon him, however: he really had no way to *start* a fire! His flint-and-steel set had been left behind in their cabin during his hasty exit, and he knew he wasn't likely to find a suitable substitute out here in the wilderness!

As he pondered the problem, a possibility occurred to him: could he perhaps create sparks by striking the blade of the metal knife against the flint of the tomahawk Wawoka had given him? It was worth a try! Geoffry gathered some soft dry moss from the side of a tree trunk, along with a supply of pine needles and small twigs, and set about testing his theory.

Time after time he struck the back of the blade against the flint, but to no avail. Changing angles, changing velocity, he tried again and again. Then just as he was beginning to despair, he experienced success! A single spark floated down from the tomahawk toward his little collection of kindling. But before it could catch fire, before Geoffry could lean close to blow it gently to life, the tiny ember died.

But now that he knew it was possible, Geoffry continued striking until at last a second spark fell amongst the bits of moss, glowed for an instant, then burst into a wisp of flame. Nursing this promising beginning with utmost care, he added more small bits of wood, then gradually larger pieces until he had a steady, dependable fire. Finally he spitted his meat on a sharpened stick and roasted it slowly over the hot coals, savoring the tantalizing aroma. His hope was that, by its sacrifice, the little animal would provide him enough strength and sustenance to push on toward his still undetermined goal.

Having completed his meal, Geoffry once again took to the trail, buoyed in both body and spirit. His journey followed much the same pattern as it had on the previous days, and again he traveled steadily, mile after mile, always in essentially the same direction as best he could determine by the position of the sun. His progress was slowed only when he came to a broad, slow-flowing river ~ one very much like the James. This time, though, he had no helpful natives to provide a canoe for his crossing, so he turned reluctantly westward, following the watercourse upstream. It was not too long before he noticed a decided narrowing of the riverbed, and thus encouraged he pressed on until he saw the estuary tapering down to a small stream. Here a convenient crossing had been improvised with simple stepping stones. The crossing appeared to be part of a larger, more frequented trail, and Geoffry was surprised to find that, intermingled with the tracks of woodland creatures, there were also moccasin prints!

Unsure of what to expect, yet curious about this first evidence of another human presence since leaving Wawoka and his friends, Geoffry set out along the new pathway. Gradually it curved back along the southern bank of the river, then again turned away into the forest toward the south. Exactly why he was pleased to be heading in that direction once more Geoffry wasn't sure, but he continued happily along the larger path, finding it much easier to traverse.

As the sun made its way across the sky, hour after hour Geoffry held to his course. A profusion of dogwood blossoms, along with other colorful blooms peeping from the forest floor, and the persistent chatter of brightly-colored birds flitting from tree to tree added to his pleasant sense of well-being ~ though exactly *why* he should feel happy in such an uncertain situation he couldn't have told.

A short distance from the trail, a bush covered with lush berries that looked ready for picking caught Geoffry's eye. He turned off the path and headed toward the bush, happy to find what looked like an easy lunch.

But he was stopped short, perplexed beyond words! Coming from the far side of the bush he heard an absolutely incongruous sound, totally mystifying and unreal in this woodland setting. Someone was softly humming a tune! And even more incredible, the tune was one that had been familiar to Geoffry since his early childhood: "God Save the Queen"!

What's going on here, he thought to himself? How can this be *possible?* Have I gone *insane?* His curiosity piqued beyond measure, he nevertheless remained cautious as he edged warily around the heavy bush, avoiding any misstep that might betray his presence.

Nothing, absolutely *nothing* could have been more unexpected that what came into view! There, contentedly picking berries while humming her tune, stood an incredibly beautiful young woman! Tall and slender, she was dressed in buckskin garb, yet she did not appear to be a traditional female Indian. Her hair was not the customary dark black but rather a light sun-streaked red! And her eyes, alert and lively as she selected her berries, shimmered a deep, translucent blue!

Chapter 23

▼

An involuntary gasp of surprise escaped Geoffry at this truly remarkable and extraordinary sight! Startled by the sudden sound, the woman dropped the berries she was picking and looked around, alarmed but displaying no real sign of fright. When she spotted Geoffry, her large eyes widened even further, and she reached reflexively for the bow and quiver of arrows lying at her feet. Before Geoffry could move, he found himself staring directly at the tip of a flint-tipped arrow, held steady against a taut bowstring drawn back to its fullest extent.

The tense, silent stand-off lasted for long seconds. Geoffry stood absolutely still, looking intently into those azure eyes, not sure what to do next or how to respond to end the confrontation. Slowly he raised his left hand, palm forward, and spoke in a firm voice: "Please don't shoot! I'm a friend!"

His words brought a confused expression to the woman's bronzed face. She hesitated, then slowly lowered her bow and relaxed her vigilant stance. But she continued to watch Geoffry closely, as though she too was uncertain as to what her next course of action should be.

"Wherever did you learn that *tune* you were humming just now?" Geoffry asked as he took a tentative step forward. Immediately the bow and arrow sprang back up, and he halted his approach.

Once more the woman lowered her weapon, and for the first time she spoke: "You not Lumbee." The voice was low and mellow, with no hint of fright or timidity.

"No, I'm English," Geoffry responded. "I'm a friend of Wawoka of the Pamunkeys, members of the Powhatan Confederation. He told me to look for the Lumbee tribe."

"Ah, Powhatan!" The name was obviously familiar, and merited a note of respect. But the perplexed expression returned. "Why look for Lumbee?" she asked.

"I'm really not sure. It's just what Wawoka said to do. Maybe he thought the Lumbee people would be kind to a stranger." After a brief pause, Geoffry inquired, "Are you Lumbee?"

The woman nodded. "Yes, I belong Lumbee tribe."

Geoffry still had not learned the answer to his most puzzling question, however: "Tell me, where in the world did you learn that tune you were humming just now, when I first saw you? You know, the one that goes…." he hummed a few bars of the familiar English song.

If the young woman had seemed surprised at Geoffry's unexpected appearance, hearing him repeat her little melody seemed to foster even greater amazement. Her mouth dropped open, her exquisite blue eyes glittering with incredulity. "You know tune *too?*" she queried in a tone of total wonderment. "You know tune my mother teach me, long long ago?"

"Your *mother?* You say your *mother* taught you that?" It was Geoffry's turn to be bewildered. "But how can that *be?* That's not an Indian tune! It's English!"

"Long story, from long time ago." The enchanting eyes dropped abruptly, and the woman turned away. She picked up her basket of berries, still keeping a watchful eye on Geoffry, still keeping her bow and arrows readily at hand. "Now you come village, talk to chief. We find out if you true friend." With that, she started down a narrow trail leading directly into the forest, with barely a backward glance to see if Geoffry was following.

Feeling that he had little choice but to do as he'd been told, Geoffry tagged along behind. Besides, he had to admit that he was extremely *curious* about this intriguing young woman with the self-assured manner, and he didn't really want to go on until he'd had an opportunity to find out more about her. She, on the other hand, seemed more concerned that she safely escort the strange visitor back to the confines of her village than with who he was or what he was doing in their territory.

It was only a short walk to the Lumbee village. The settlement was truly impressive, Geoffry noted as they approached. Huts constructed of reeds or swamp-grass, each with a distinctive arched roof, were spread everywhere throughout the clearing. Intermingled amongst the houses were small garden plots where he saw a variety of gourds, beans, and other vegetable crops. On the outskirts beyond, he could see a substantial cleared area covered with fields of corn, promising a stable supply of food. Everywhere people were at work, some roasting ears of corn, others grilling fish on racks over large open fires, still others using fire to hollow a huge tree trunk apparently destined to become some type of boat. Children were equally in evidence ~ running about, happily playing games, or watching adults at their work. To Geoffry it was a marvelous sight, reinforcing his belief that English settlers could indeed learn a great deal from natives such as these. All that would be necessary would be to work in peace and harmony, rather than resorting to the customary European air of perceived superiority.

Near the center of the settlement was a long low structure built in the same manner as the houses, only much larger, and Geoffry guessed it must be the tribal meeting place. In front was a cleared area containing a massive stone-ringed fire pit, surrounded by a variety of rocks and stumps suitable for seating. Just beyond the open square was another substantial-looking shelter, somewhat isolated, and it was toward this structure that the young woman appeared to be directing Geoffry.

Natives greeted the woman respectfully as the pair passed, with curious sidelong glances cast at Geoffry. She did not halt, however, until they reached the larger hut, where she signaled him to wait. Her call brought an elderly Indian to the door ~ his posture tall and erect, his face deeply lined, his long white hair held back by a shell-encrusted ornament. His dignified carriage even more than his elaborate imperial regalia made it obvious that he was a leader, a personage of authority. On seeing the young woman who had summoned him, the man broke into a warm smile of welcome and the two embraced affectionately as they exchanged greetings.

When the man's eyes settled on Geoffry, his demeanor immediately turned serious and he spoke to the woman with a stern, questioning edge to his voice. As she replied, still only in their native tongue, the man's glance shifted between Geoffry and the woman. Then he stepped forward to confront Geoffry, looking directly into his eyes as the woman explained, "This my father, Lagoda, chief of Lumbee tribe."

Giving a slight bow, Geoffry extended his hand. "Greetings, Chief Lagoda of the Lumbees. I am Geoffry Payne, Englishman, friend of Wawoka of the Pamunkeys, members of the Powhatan Confederation."

The chief's face remained impassive as he gripped the proffered hand, but at mention of Powhatan his eyebrows raised slightly and he appeared to relax. Turning to his daughter, he spoke briefly, then waited for her to translate: "Father ask why you come to Lumbee tribe."

"Tell your father that I was forced to leave the English settlement at James' Towne. Wawoka suggested that I seek the villages of the Croatoans or the Lumbees, friends of the Pamunkey. So here I am!"

It took some time as native words were exchanged before the young woman again turned to Geoffry: "Father ask *why* you must go from English settlement."

"Tell him that I was falsely accused by a powerful enemy and was sentenced to be hanged, so I fled."

A quizzical expression came over the woman's face, and she shook her head: "Not understand."

Geoffry tried to clarify: "I was accused of stealing food, and was sentenced to death."

This time she nodded, then once more relayed the information to the chief. Lagoda looked sharply at Geoffry, and another rapid exchange of native words ensued. At the conclusion, Chief Lagoda contemplated for a moment before again extending his hand to Geoffry. "Welcome, Geoffry Payne," he said, then turned and disappeared into his dwelling.

Caught by surprise at Lagoda's welcome, Geoffry looked questioningly at the chief's daughter. She tried to appear nonchalant, but the soft smile that brightened her face, along with the sparkle in her eyes, betrayed her.

"Father say you not look like thief," she explained with obvious pleasure. "You stay with Lumbee."

Geoffry's face also lighted in a warm grin at her words, and he breathed a sigh of deep relief. "Thank you very much, both you and your father. Wawoka was right: the Lumbees truly *are* friends!"

He extended his hand, and the young woman quickly grasped it. Geoffry felt a thrill at its softness in his own work-callused one, yet he could also feel its strength. Continuing his hold for a bit longer, Geoffry added gently, "You haven't even told me your name yet."

"My name Priscilla," she replied, her brilliant eyes looking deeply into his own. Slowly she withdrew her hand.

"Priscilla!" Geoffry mused for a moment. "It's a very pretty name, but not one I'd really expect to find among the native people here. Did Chief Lagoda choose that name for you?"

She emitted a melodic little laugh. "No, not chief." She paused as though uncertain just how much to relate. "Someday Priscilla tell," she finished. Almost immediately she reverted to her previous businesslike manner. "Father say you stay in empty house over there," she pointed toward a hut near the edge of the clearing. "Come, I show you." Without looking back, she led the way, then stopped at the entrance and indicated the dwelling: "This your place now, Geoffry Payne." Again the warm smile and friendly eyes projected a special note.

"Thank you, Priscilla, and please thank Chief Lagoda for me, too. I'll be very happy here!"

As she turned to leave, Geoffry added, "I hope we can talk some more soon, Priscilla. I still have lots of questions to ask you ~ like where a young woman like you learned to use a bow and arrow. Or how you learned to speak English. And especially how you learned that tune you were humming!" Again he hummed a few notes from the familiar melody.

A delighted laugh broke from the young woman. "We talk again, Geoffry Payne," she replied, then started back toward her own dwelling with a light spring in her step.

Chapter 24

▼

Geoffry watched until Priscilla disappeared from view. Still feeling a warm inner glow, he turned and entered his new shelter. The hut was comprised of one simple room containing a low bed made of rushes and dried grasses, a few shelves along one wall holding some decorated baskets, and a stool fashioned from an old stump. Still, as he looked around, Geoffry felt a calm and serenity he had not experienced since he and Billy completed their own little home back at James Fort.

He spread his buckskin blanket on the bed, placed his knife and tomahawk on an empty shelf, and after putting what was left of his meager food supply on another shelf, stepped outside to check the surroundings. Two children playing nearby stopped their game to edge in for a closer look at the stranger, making sure they still remained at a safe distance. When Geoffry greeted them in English, they smiled shyly but did not respond or venture nearer. He went inside and picked two small strips of pemmican from his now almost-depleted store, then went back out and held up the jerky in one hand while giving the sign of peace with the other. The smaller of the two children, a little boy clad only in a buckskin breech-cloth, was urged forward by his sister and approached step by cautious step until he was close enough to reach out and accept the pemmican. He retreated quickly to the safety of his sister's side, shared a strip with her, then turned to give Geoffry a quick smile of thanks and a brief wave before running off, his sister following close behind.

Well, maybe I've managed to make a couple of friends, Geoffry thought, even if they are rather small ones. But sharing the pemmican reminded him once more that he really had very little food of any sort left. With evening approaching, however, he decided he would probably have to wait until morning to try to replenish his stock.

As he stood gazing around at his new environs, he was pleasantly surprised to see Priscilla again approaching his residence. She was carrying a basket covered with a reed mat. She handed the basket to Geoffry with her usual engaging smile and stated, "You need food. Need to eat, then rest."

"Why, thank you, Priscilla! That's really very kind of you. And you're right, I was just thinking that I'm going to have to do some hunting soon because my food supply has run so low. Thank you very much!"

She smiled in response and turned to go. Not yet willing to have her leave, Geoffry added, "Would you like to join me? Maybe we could talk some more that way, while we eat."

Priscilla laughed lightly and shook her head. "Already eat. But maybe I show you where to hunt tomorrow. We talk then."

"That would be just great, Priscilla," Geoffry responded with genuine enthusiasm. "I'd really like that!"

"Then I see you in morning." With another bright smile, she left to return to her own home.

Geoffry's spirits soared at the prospect of seeing more of this enigmatic young woman and perhaps getting better acquainted. He watched until she disappeared, then checked the basket to see what she had brought. It contained a gourd bowl filled with a mixture of cooked meat, beans, and pine nuts, as well as a piece of corn bread and some fresh berries ~ probably those he'd seen her pick earlier that day, Geoffry concluded happily. It was certainly a huge improvement over what he'd been subsisting on during the past few days, and he consumed the meal with relish. As dusk fell quietly over the Lumbee village, a contented Geoffry stretched out on his new bed under his buckskin blanket and drifted off to a land of pleasant dreams.

At first light of day Geoffry awoke, eager and full of anticipation. He had seen a rather large, broad river beyond the fields at the edge of the settlement when they arrived, and he now headed there to wash up. Even at this early hour, several groups of natives were already gathered along the stream fishing with nets, and he decided that this might prove to be a good additional means for him to augment his own depleted store of food.

When he returned to his hut, he was delighted to see Priscilla already there, waiting outside with another basket in hand. "Good morning, Priscilla, how very nice to see you again!" he greeted her with a wide grin. "You're up pretty early, aren't you?"

She responded with her melodic laugh. "Need to start early to hunt," she informed him. "But first you eat."

"If this is as good as last night's dinner, I'll be only too happy to eat first," he replied, checking the basket. It held another slice of cornbread, more berries, an egg, and a piece of meat that looked very much like the breakfast ham he had always enjoyed so much back in Salisbury.

"What *is* this?" he asked, indicating the meat.

"That wild boar meat. There, boiled duck egg. Now you eat," she smiled at his enthusiasm.

While Geoffry enjoyed his morning repast, Priscilla checked her quiver of arrows, along with the tension of her bowstring. "You have bow and arrows?" she inquired.

"No, all I have is the tomahawk and knife that Wawoka gave me. But your question reminds me of one of the things I wanted to ask you: Where did you ever learn to *use* a bow and arrow, anyway? Or are all Lumbee women hunters, like you seem to be?'

His query evoked another tinkling laugh. "No, Lumbee women not hunt. Men hunt, women care for children, all work together in fields."

"But you seem to…." Geoffry was still puzzled.

She laughed again. "Yes, I know how shoot bow and arrow. Chief Lagoda have no son, so teach *me*. I try and try, now can shoot straight." An almost-forgotten recollection brought a mischievous twinkle to her eyes: "Sometimes shoot better than boys, scare them away."

Geoffry joined in her laughter. But he also privately determined to leave the intricacies of hunting with bow and arrow to Priscilla, at least until he could achieve enough proficiency in their use to avoid embarrassment.

As he finished his breakfast, Geoffry remarked, "That was really good! Did you bake that cornbread?"

"Yes, I bake," Priscilla flushed a bit at the praise, obviously pleased. "Learn from watch mother, long ago." A wistful shadow crossed her face.

"Well, that leads me to a second question," Geoffry interjected. "You told me yesterday that you learned to speak English from your mother. How could that be? Can you tell me how all that happened?"

Priscilla lowered her eyes and was silent for a few moments, as though drifting back mentally to another time. Then she rose abruptly. "Better to hunt now, talk later." She shouldered her weapons and started off toward the woods. "You come," she called back.

Retrieving his knife and tomahawk from the shelf in his hut, Geoffry hurried after the young woman, who seemed to know precisely where she wanted to go. They moved quietly down a half-hidden trail in single file, alert, eyes roaming from side to side as they went.

Nothing caught their attention until the trail curved around toward the river. Then, as they approached a small clearing close to the water, Priscilla stopped and looked back, placing a finger to her lips. Step by step, with great caution they edged closer, until Geoffry spotted their quarry just ahead: a flock of wild geese, feeding on grubs and grass in the little clearing.

Priscilla pointed toward one large goose ~ its head held high, its eyes scanning the landscape ~ who appeared to be the appointed look-out for the flock. Silently, with calm, unhurried motions, she pulled an arrow from her quiver and placed it in her bow, drew the bow back in a sure, steady movement, and sent the arrow on its way. Alerted too late, the sentry goose emitted one loud squawk of warning before the arrow found its mark. The rest of the flock rose in a flurry of noisy wing-flapping and fled to the safety of the river, but not the sentinel. Once again, it seemed, "the law of the jungle" had decreed that one be sacrificed so that others may survive.

"Great shot, Priscilla!" Geoffry called out in a hushed tone. "You really are good with that thing, aren't you?" Priscilla looked at him with a slight smile of appreciation, then rose to retrieve her prize. She pulled out the fatal arrow, but a look of sadness at the cruelty essential for human subsistence shadowed her beautiful eyes. She grasped the dead goose by its feet, handed it to Geoffry, and said, "Come, we go back now."

Both were silent until they reached Geoffry's little hut, where they set about preparing the bird for cooking. But something from his days back home in Salisbury flashed through Geoffry's mind, and he said, "Just a minute, Priscilla. I'd like to save these feathers." He brought out one of the large baskets from his dwelling. Then, sitting on a stump with the goose held firmly between his knees, he began plucking the breast feathers, a handful at a time, and dropping them into the basket. "These should make a great pillow," he told her. "At least that's what my grandmother back in England used when she made them."

Priscilla watched as he worked, curious but seemingly uncertain as to what he had in mind. When he had picked all of the usable feathers, Geoffry explained, "I'll have to make myself a buckskin bag first. Then all I have to do is stuff it full of these feathers and I'll have a grand pillow, just like back home." She laughed, still apparently unsure of what he was talking about but taking pleasure in his happy anticipation.

After cleaning the bird thoroughly, Priscilla set it aside while she dug a shallow pit in the ground and lined it with rocks. She placed the goose on the stones, remarking "I come back soon," and hurried off in the direction of her own home. In a few minutes she was back, carrying a lighted firebrand which she handed to Geoffry. She also brought some large green leaves, more cornbread, and a small basket of mixed vegetables ~ green beans, shelled corn, and a tuberous root she said was a yam. The vegetables and cornbread were cut up and stuffed inside the goose. Next she wrapped the goose with the green leaves and finally covered everything with more stones and a light layer of earth.

"Now we build fire," she informed Geoffry as she set a ring of rocks around the top of the pit she had dug. Inside this ring she placed kindling and twigs, which she lighted with the firebrand, gradually adding larger pieces of wood until she had a hot, slow-burning fire.

"Now we wait, Geoffry Payne," she said, apparently satisfied with her preparations. "When goose cooked, we eat. While we wait, we talk."

Chapter 25

▼

"It time to tell about mother, father," Priscilla began. "Long story."

"I don't mind how long it is," Geoffry assured her. "I want to find out absolutely everything I can about you and your background, so just take your time."

"You say you English? My mother, father English too." She paused briefly at the look of surprise in Geoffry's eyes, then went on: "Before she die, mother tell me many times story how they come across big water to start new life in new land. Sell everything they have in England, come on big boat. Leader man promise much land, so they come. Settle at place called Roanoke."

"*Roanoke?* You mean they came to Roanoke Island?" Geoffry could not contain his astonishment. "Then you must be part of the 'Lost Colony'!"

"Why you say 'Lost Colony'? We not lost!"

"But everyone back home thought the whole *colony* was either killed or died of disease or something. No one ever found any survivors."

"Well, we *not* lost! We know where we are. We right *here!* You just not find us!"

"But how can that *be?* Captain Smith and lots of others looked *everywhere* for survivors of the colony!"

"Not look *everywhere!* Maybe look some places, but not look with Lumbee tribe. We *here!*"

"But do you remember how you came to *be* here with the Lumbees? Or why your family *left* Roanoke Island? How did all that happen?"

"Long story, like I say. Mother tell me. She say I must remember my hair…my hara…" Priscilla halted, searching for the correct word.

"You mean your 'heritage'?"

"Yes, yes, that right word! I forget! But I not forget story, even if I only little girl then."

"How old *were* you when you came to the Lumbee village, Priscilla? Or were you born here, after your parents joined the Lumbees? Do you remember all of that?"

She laughed at his rapid-fire questions and his curiosity. "I tell you, but must go slow. Forget many words of English. Have no one to talk to after while, so learn Lumbee language instead. But I tell what I remember."

Geoffry settled back, determined not to interrupt in spite of the many questions that surged through his mind. Priscilla took a deep breath and continued her story: "Mother say we part of *second* people come to Roanoke. First people go back to England, leave only fort and some soldiers. When our people come, she say fort burned, soldiers dead. New people build new fort. Want to start farms, like back home. But too late in year to plant, so have no food. Finally leader man named Gov…Gover…"

"Governor?"

"Yes, governor!" Priscilla smiled her appreciation. "Governor White, he leader man. He say he go back home, get more food. He go, we wait ~ wait long, long time. Never come back."

"Yes, I remember my parents talking about that, years ago. They said Governor White had come back to England and was trying to raise money to buy supplies to take to his colony. But then the Spanish Armada came, and everyone just sort of *forgot* about the colony."

"We not know what happen, only know Gov…Governor never come back, so have no food."

Priscilla went on, explaining how her mother had told her that the local Indian tribes refused to help the new colonists because the natives had been so badly mistreated by the *first* group of settlers at Roanoke: an entire Indian village had been burned and their crops destroyed because one native was suspected of stealing a silver cup. As a result, starvation and illness soon began taking their toll on the new Roanoke colonists, until finally those still surviving decided to leave Roanoke Island to search for food. These survivors were divided into three groups: one would go south to seek help from the Croatoans, who had proved friendly earlier; another would move north to the area around the great bay ~ the place where the whole entourage had hoped to settle in the first place; and the third group would try their luck on the mainland directly west of Roanoke Island. Her parents were part of this last contingent, she said, and this was the group that had been taken in by the Lumbee tribe.

"Mother say they walk through woods, walk many days, look for food. Father have to carry me, only four years old. Many people get sick on way and die. Father try hard to care for us, but then he get sick, soon he die too. Mother, few others keep going. Finally last of people found by Lumbee hunters, almost dead. Bring all to Lumbee village. Chief Lagoda ~ yes, he chief then, too, only much younger ~ take people in, give food, make houses. Very kind man. So Roanoke people stay with Lumbees. Not 'lost' at all, like you think!"

She looked at Geoffry somewhat defiantly, but his rapt attention as well as his look of deep sympathy softened her attitude. She smiled, seeing that he could hardly wait to pose more questions.

"So you and your mother both lived with the Lumbees? For how long? Were there many other colonists with you? And how did you come to lose your mother? What happened?"

Priscilla laughed, but with a note of sadness. "You ask many questions, Geoffry Payne! I try tell you. Mother live maybe two, three more years. Make me speak English, like other English children. But finally other Roanoke people leave, want to find relatives who go to big bay. We stay. So I play with Lumbee children, learn Lumbee words.

"One day, mother come home from fields, not feel well. Feel very hot, like burning with fire. I get chief Lagoda, but he can do nothing. After she die, Chief Lagoda say he take care of me, say I now his daughter. He very good man, good to all people," she ended her account.

"That's an *incredible* story, Priscilla! I'm so glad you told me! And I especially appreciate what Chief Lagoda did. Otherwise, you really *could* have been 'lost,' couldn't you?" He hesitated, then looked intently into her extraordinary blue eyes as he told her with deep, heart-felt emotion: "I'm awfully happy that you survived, Priscilla, and that you're here ~ and that I *found* you, safe with the Lumbees!" He couldn't control the tears that welled in his eyes.

Priscilla seemed moved by the intensity of his feelings and responded with a radiant smile. Geoffry had to exercise every measure of his self-control to keep from taking the delightful young woman into his arms to comfort and cherish her. Instead, he reached out and gently touched her hand. "Thank you for telling me your story, Priscilla. It means a lot to me!"

The tender exchange brought a warm light to Priscilla's eyes as she added a detail she had neglected during her narration: "Now you know how I learn song you hear by berry bush," she said with her lyrical laugh. "Mother sing song many times, say it honor 'good Queen Bess.' I not know who Queen Bess is, not know words, but remember tune."

"Well, I'll have to admit that it *did* come as quite a surprise to hear that tune out there in the middle of a wild forest! But it got me acquainted with *you*, Priscilla, and that's about the nicest thing that's ever happened to me!"

She lowered her eyes, visibly embarrassed, yet she could not hide a smile of pleasure. To cover her self-consciousness, she posed her own questions: "So, I tell you all I remember about coming to Lumbees, Geoffry Payne. Now, you tell *me*: how *you* come *here?* Why you come this land? Where you stay? Why you all alone out in woods?"

Geoffry couldn't restrain a chuckle at how cleverly she had turned the tables. "That's fair enough, I guess. But first, please, you don't have to keep calling me 'Geoffry Payne.' Payne is my *last* name. So if you just call me 'Geoffry,' I'd like that very much."

"What means 'last name'? Name not Geoffry Payne?"

"Yes, it is, but usually when people get to know each other better, they use only their *first* names, like 'Geoffry.' Your first name is Priscilla. Didn't you have a last name before you came here?"

For some moments Priscilla was quiet, deep in thought. Then she brightened. "Sometimes when I little girl, if I do bad thing, mother say, 'Priscilla Ann Weatherford, you stop that!' Could *that* be last name?"

Geoffry could not restrain a laugh, both at her earnestness and at the seeming universality of the familiar custom. "Yes, that must be your full name: Priscilla Ann Weatherford. And I remember my mother doing exactly the same thing to me when I misbehaved."

Priscilla was not to be put off, however. "Now, Geoffry, you tell me how you get here, like I tell."

"I'm afraid my story isn't nearly as exciting as yours, Priscilla." Still, he related a general summary of his own experiences, both on the way to Virginia and in the establishment of the James' Towne settlement. He included the role played by Captain John Smith as well as that of Billy Bascomb, and how it was Billy's sacrificial effort that had enabled him to escape almost certain death. "And the rest you know, since you're the one who brought me here," he concluded.

Her blue eyes sparkled with interest at his tale. "Captain Smith, Billy Bascomb good men, good friends, yes?"

"They certainly were, both of them. If Captain Smith hadn't got hurt, I really think the James' Towne colony might have done quite well. Now, I'm not sure *what* will happen. And Billy was truly a very, very special friend!" Geoffry hesitated, recalling his obligation. "I still have to figure out some way to get a letter to Billy's mother back in London, too. I *promised!*"

"You find way, Geoffry, you keep promise," Priscilla assured him. But another element of his narration seemed to intrigue her: "You say other English people still live here? Live in own village at, how you say…James' Towne? Not with Lumbee or Powhatan or Croatoan tribes?"

"No, the English live separately. They hope to establish permanent settlements all along the coast so they can farm and trade and send products back home to England." Priscilla appeared puzzled by this explanation, so Geoffry attempted to clarify: "The English came here to find gold and silver and other riches, just like the Spanish did. But so far they haven't found any, so now they plan to send back wood from the forests, and pitch, and fish, and things like that instead. Some Englishmen want to build farms over here, too, like they had at home, and then send their extra food to sell back in England. There's so much land over here, for farming or whatever, it seems just endless!"

"Yes, much land. Enough for *everyone*, if people share. But must use land well, not destroy."

"That's a lesson I really hope we learn from your people," Geoffry agreed. "But I'm afraid the problem might be that the English will *refuse* to share and just try to take the land for themselves."

"How they 'take' land? Where they put it?" Priscilla seemed genuinely confused by the European concept of land ownership. "Land not belong one person. Land belong to all, to *everybody*!"

"We do have a lot to learn from you, Priscilla. And sooner or later, I'm afraid land ownership is going to cause a lot of trouble between our two peoples." Geoffry could only hope that a harmonious outcome would evolve, but was not optimistic.

For now, however, there were far more positive prospects in store, and he determined not to let any worries about the future dim them. "I'm really happy that you remember so much of your old language, Priscilla, so that we can communicate with each other like this. Otherwise, I might never have learned about your background and how you ended up here with the Lumbee tribe and everything."

A further thought flashed through Geoffry's mind ~ one with far-reaching possibilities: "Do you suppose there might be some way in the future that you and I could *help* with that communication problem, Priscilla? You know the Lumbee language and you know English. Maybe I can learn to speak your language, too, and then we could help our two people to talk to each other, to try to better understand one another, instead of always being suspicious and fighting! Wouldn't that be great?"

Catching Geoffry's sense of excitement, Priscilla exclaimed, "You good man, Geoffry Pa.... um, Geoffry, just like Chief Lagoda. You both try make all people happy. Try make all *world* happy! Maybe I can help, but first need learn better English again. You help me?"

"I'd be *delighted* to help you any way I can, Priscilla, even though your English sounds perfectly fine to me. I guess we'll just have to keep talking to each other to give you more practice, that's all." Both enjoyed a laugh at Geoffry's not-too-subtle hint at a continuing relationship.

"Enough talk for now, Geoffry," Priscilla informed him. "Time to dig up goose from pit, and eat!"

Chapter 26

▼

* * * * *
-Three Years Later-
* * * * *

"I think we'd better get started, Priscilla. Too late to change our minds now, I'm afraid!"

"I know, Geoffry, but I can't help being a little worried, wondering what's ahead for us. It's been such a long time since I was in England, and we're used to living a totally different life here, peaceful and quiet. I'm just not sure I'm ready for a big busy city like London."

"We won't be there long, I promise! Then we'll come right back to these familiar surroundings, just as soon as we can." Geoffry gazed lovingly into Priscilla's large dazzling blue eyes ~ eyes that never ceased to amaze or charm him ~ and he held her close. "Thank you again for agreeing to go with me on this voyage, Sweetheart! I know it's scary, but we'll be *together*, and as long as we're together nothing in the *world* can be too much for us to handle!"

They said a last goodbye to Chief Lagoda, with Priscilla reassuring the old leader once more in the Lumbee language that they would be back as quickly as possible. The chief's deeply creased face softened in a slight smile at her words, but his perceptive dark eyes harbored a hint of doubt, as though he were afraid this parting might be a final farewell.

As they left the village, the young couple turned several times to wave to the lonely figure watching their departure, until finally he was lost to sight as they moved around a bend in the forest path, the trail that would lead them to the coast. It was a well-marked route, used frequently now by natives to transport goods they planned to trade as well as by traders who on occasion brought their wares directly to the village.

"So much has *changed* these past few years, hasn't it, Priscilla?" Geoffry remarked as they followed the trail. "It's hard to believe that just three years ago your Lumbee village was almost completely isolated. Now your people take trade goods to ships that make regular stops all along the coast. And other villages do the same thing."

Geoffry stopped suddenly, struck by a thought: "Do you suppose *that's* how we could help the native people here, Priscilla ~ by making sure they don't get *cheated* in their trading? We know both languages pretty well now, thanks to your patience in helping me to learn Lumbee, and you seem to be much more comfortable with your English. Maybe we could act kind of like 'interpreters,' so that everyone who's trading goods knows what's being said and no one takes advantage of anyone else. Does that sound reasonable?"

It took only a moment for Priscilla to get caught up in both Geoffry's vision and his enthusiasm. "Oh yes, Geoffry, I think we really *could* be helpful that way!" she agreed. "Maybe we could set up a sort of 'trading place' where people from both sides could bring their goods, and then make sure everyone is treated fairly when they trade. Oh, I'd really *like* being able to help the people who helped *me* so much!"

The two walked on chatting excitedly for a time before Geoffry stopped again and turned to Priscilla, looking tenderly into her remarkable eyes: "But of everything that's happened, you know what's still hardest for me to believe? It's that you really truly are my *wife* now!"

Priscilla emitted one of her tinkling laughs as she snuggled against Geoffry's chest. "Poor Chief Lagoda! Remember, he wasn't too *happy* at first when you asked to marry me, was he? He didn't seem too sure about someone who'd been accused of stealing food!" She smiled up at Geoffry, her radiant eyes aglow. "But you won him over, just like you did me! And then when he even agreed to perform our marriage ceremony, that was so special!" A wistful note crept into her voice. "I hope he'll be all right while we're gone, Geoffry. He's really been a father to me ever since my mother died."

"I'm sure he'll be just fine," Geoffry reassured her. "All of the village women promised to take turns cooking for him and looking after him. Who knows, maybe he'll even *marry* one of them before we get back," Geoffry concluded with a laugh.

The mood of friendly banter and camaraderie continued as they followed the path toward the coast. Their travel time was providing a perfect opportunity to reminisce, as well as for Priscilla to voice some of her lingering concerns: "Oh Geoffry, I still don't know if I'm ready for all the new things ahead of us. I really don't want to embarrass you in any way! But I know how much you need to keep your promise to your friend Billy Bascomb. And I know how much you want to see your family again, too, after all these years, so I'll do my best."

"You'll be *wonderful*, Priscilla, just exactly the way you are! And I'm glad you understand how important it is for me to finally contact Billy's Mum and let her know everything that happened. I've been wanting to write to her for a long, long time, but paper and pen and ink are pretty scarce among the Lumbees, as you know ~ a lot like their whole postal system," he grinned at his understatement. "This way, we can make a real all-out effort to find Mum Bascomb in London, if she's still alive, and then I can tell her *personally* just how much Billy talked about her, and how much he loved and admired her. After that, we'll head for Salisbury for a little visit before we come back here ~ to what's our *real* home now. I'm so anxious for my family to meet you, Priscilla!"

Her large eyes reflected a new uncertainty. "Do you think they'll really like me, Geoffry? Me, who's what they'd probably call a 'wild Indian,' or a 'savage'?"

Geoffry took the delightful woman that was his wife into his arms, holding her as tightly as he dared. "They're going to *love* you, Priscilla, just wait and see! How could they *help* themselves, as beautiful as you are, and with all of your charm and graciousness?" He chuckled as he added, "I'm afraid the big problem might be that they'll never want you to *leave* Salisbury to come back with me, back here where we truly belong."

Priscilla laughed brightly at his confidence. "Well, there is still that *other* problem we haven't solved," she reminded him. "Are you *sure* we'll be able to find proper English clothes to wear before we get there? If we show up at your home in these buckskins, with your hair in that long braid and everything, they'll probably think we really *are* a couple of 'savages.'"

Her assessment brought a wide grin to Geoffry's face, but he also sensed her unease. "If I know anything about a bunch of sailors," he told her, "I'm sure that at least *one* of them will have a dress he picked up somewhere for a girlfriend that he'd be willing to sell me at a nice profit. In fact, he'd probably sell me his naval uniform and all of his own clothes if I offer him enough money. So I think we'll be fine. If not, we can always buy new things in London, before we go on to Salisbury."

"That's another thing: can we really use those smooth little round stones you call 'pearls' to pay for our passage on the ship, and to buy what we need in England? Can they truly be as *valuable* as you've been telling me?" She looked quizzically at Geoffry. "You know from living with my people that when they find 'pearls' like those in the oysters they gather, they usually just throw them away."

"Well, I'm certainly glad you ended up *saving* quite a few of them, and that we've been able to *add* to that collection during these past years. Yes, believe me, they're *very* valuable. Men have killed to get them! Hopefully we can sell enough pearls to buy whatever we need ~ that is, if we can keep the sailors aboard from *stealing* them first," Geoffry said, only half in jest. "We'll have to be careful to keep our little pouch of pearls well hidden, and bring out just a few at a time when we need to pay for something. We don't want anyone to know just how 'rich' we really are, do we?" he finished with a laugh.

Each remained absorbed in private thoughts for a time, until Priscilla touched Geoffry's arm softly and asked, "Do you ever wonder what happened to that little house you told me about, the one you and Billy built back in James' Towne? You know, with the stone floor and fireplace?" She smiled up at him. "It sounded so nice!"

Geoffry grinned in response. "Yes, I *have* thought about it ~ quite often, to tell the truth! And you know, it's just possible we may be able to find out if it's still there."

"Really? How's that, Geoffry?"

"From what I was told, trading ships make pretty regular stops all along the coast now, and sometimes they actually stop right at James' Towne. So if our ship *does* happen to stop there, maybe we'll have a chance to slip ashore and see if we can find out what happened to our old home! I'd really like to see it again, Priscilla." With a chuckle, he added, "Of course, our plans could change in a hurry if old Gabriel Archer's still around!"

"You mean that lawyer you told me about? The one who gave you so much trouble, and accused you of stealing food? You don't suppose he *could* still be in James' Towne, do you?"

"For the good of the colony, I certainly *hope* not! If Archer didn't die during the 'starving time,' though, I suspect he's gone back home to England by now, where life is much easier. But that shyster was real trouble!"

It was about a week later when Priscilla and Geoffry stood hand in hand at the railing of a trading ship as it moved slowly upstream against the languid current of the James River. They wore the attire of two typical English travelers ~ clothes Geoffry had been successful in acquiring from a willing sailor, just as he had predicted. Priscilla, a bit self-conscious in her new blue silk gown with its delicate ruffles and lace, a matching hat, plus elegant new shoes, constantly drew admiring glances from passing members of the crew. For himself, Geoffry had managed to obtain a dark blue waistcoat, buff colored breeches and vest, and tall black boots.

When they booked passage on the trader, the ship's captain had informed the young couple that, yes, their vessel *would* be making additional stops to take on cargo, and one stop would indeed be at what he called "that thriving little colony of Jamestown." They could scarcely contain their excitement at the news! Now here they were, approaching the familiar site from which Geoffry had been forced to flee three years earlier.

"I can't *believe* how much everything's *changed* here, Priscilla! There are so many things *going on!* When I left, the colony was barely surviving. Now everything is so *different!* It's hard to imagine! About all I recognize is good old James Fort itself!"

Geoffry continued to survey the new developments. Recently built houses, some still uncompleted, again lined a makeshift street outside the palisades. Fields and garden plots were planted and being tended to insure a steady food supply. He noticed something else as well: "Look there, just ahead of us, Priscilla. They've built a whole new dock! And there are two other trading ships already tied up to it. I can't believe it! People seem to be just *everywhere!*"

"Oh Geoffry, I'm so happy that we get to make this stop! I was truly *hoping* we'd be able to come back here, and maybe even see your little home again!"

"I'm still not totally sure that's such a good idea, Priscilla. Old Archer really *could* still be around! I'll have to be very careful until I find out, because he'd still keep trying to have me hanged, you can bet on that! Archer *never* forgot an insult!"

The two were caught up in the hustle and bustle of landing as the trading ship was secured to the dock. It would be a brief stop, they were told, only long enough to take on the huge stack of barrels waiting on the pier.

"What's *in* all of those barrels, anyway, Geoffry?" Priscilla wanted to know. "I thought the ship was pretty well loaded already."

"I'm really not sure *what* it could be. Maybe we can ask one of the sailors."

A talkative young tar proved only too happy to display his knowledge for the inquisitive pair. "Them there's hogsheads, they is. They holds tabaccah," he informed them. "We been pickin' up tabaccah at every stop we makes, an' we *still* never seems to get enough o' the stuff. There's a right terrific market for tabaccah back in England right now, there is."

"But what do they *do* with all of it?" Geoffry wanted to know.

"Why, they smokes it, they does, in pipes, or they makes it into snuff to stuff up their noses. Seems like 'bout *everyone's* got the habit by now! And I heard it's got the king mighty unhappy, too, it has!"

"What do you mean?"

"Ol' King James calls tabaccah 'that stinkin' weed,' he does. Says it's 'harmful to the brain and dangerous to the lungs.' But leastwise that stinkin' weed's made Jamestown into a colony what's makin' lots o' money, as you can plainly see."

"You mean all they do here now is raise *tobacco*? What about the glass works and the iron foundry and the naval products and all of that? Has tobacco really become more important that all those other things?"

"Oh yeah! No one seems to want to do none o' them other jobs no more. Once them settlers found how much money they could make raisin' tabaccah, that's all anyone wants to do. Why, I understands they's even plowed up some o' the streets in the settlement, they has, just to have more cleared space for raisin' tabaccah."

Geoffry was mystified by the unending activity he saw all around, with settlers and sailors bustling about in their haste to load the precious new cargo. "How did all this come about, anyway? It seems to have happened so *fast*! Last I remember, the colonists were barely hanging on, and it looked like everyone here might actually *starve* to death."

"Yeah," replied the sailor, "from what I heard tell, the whole settlement dang near come apart there for a spell, it did. People was dyin' everywheres, and finally all them what was left decided to just give up and go on back to England. They was even startin' down river, lookin' for a ship to go on, they was. But right about then, accordin' to what I was told, three ships from England showed up, and they brung extra supplies, and they even brung a new governor, Lord De La Warr or somethin' like that. And I reckon this new governor was plenty tough, he was, 'cause he finally got people to workin' again, an' all, and ol' Jamestown up an' made 'er after all!"

"But I still don't understand what makes smoking tobacco so *popular*. Captain Smith used to smoke a pipe sometimes, using native tobacco, and he always said it tasted really strong and kind of bitter. So why would people want to take up a habit like *that?*"

"Oh, I sees what ya means," their new acquaintance responded, "and I thinks I can explain. See, there was this feller in Jamestown, from what I heard, name o'

John Rolfe what figgered a way to make tabaccah taste a whole lot better, not so harsh. I hears he brung some new kinda tabaccah seeds from Bermuda or somewheres. Then, when his tabaccah plants was growed, 'stead o' just throwin' the leaves on big piles to dry, he hung 'em up on racks, he did, up off the ground so's they'd dry natcheral-like in the air. Seems it made the tabaccah taste a lot milder, and afore ya knew it, everyone wanted to get in on the new smokin' craze, they did. Yesiree!"

"You say a man named John Rolfe started it all? I vaguely remember that name, though I'm not real sure. I think he may have come over with that 'Third Supply.' But I didn't know if he survived the 'starving time' or not. He certainly did change Jamestown, though, didn't he?"

"Yeah, that he did, for sure! And did ya' know the *bestest* part about ol' Rolfe? He up and married 'im a gen-u-wine Injun princess, he did! Yesiree! Name o' Pocahantas, and 'most as pretty as your *own* beauteous princess here." He eyed Priscilla appreciatively, indicating full approval of her appearance in her new attire.

"John Rolfe married *Pocahantas?* Really? Remember, Priscilla, I told you about her. Pocahantas is Powhatan's daughter, the one who saved Captain Smith's life. So she ended up marrying Rolfe instead of the Captain! Well, well! Now that's a real surprise!"

By this time, passengers had been given permission to leave the ship briefly, with strict orders to return at the proper hour to board again or risk being left behind. Geoffry and Priscilla thanked the genial young sailor warmly for all of his information, then disembarked with the others.

"We'll have to hurry if we want to see what happened to that little house of ours. It wasn't very far from here, but we sure don't want to be late getting back, do we?"

The short walk through the familiar gates of the fort and past the cluttered interior grounds took only minutes. As they reached the area to the rear of the fort, Geoffry gave a sudden exuberant cry, startling Priscilla: "Hey, *there it is!* It's still standing! Will you look at that? And it looks just like it did when I left!"

Sure enough, the little house he and Billy had constructed with such care was not only standing but appeared to be as snug and serviceable as ever.

"Shall we see if we can get a quick peek inside?" Geoffry asked. "This really is something, isn't it?"

Priscilla clutched Geoffry's arm tightly, sharing his pleasure and excitement. "Oh Geoffry, I'm so glad it's still here! What a pretty place! It looks so sturdy! No wonder it survived."

As they approached the door, Geoffry halted, pointing to a sign over the entry: "Commandant of James Fort."

"Will you look at *that!*" A note of pride crept into Geoffry's voice. "Our little house seems to have become the *headquarters* for the commander of the fort! Wow! I'm sure Billy would be mighty proud to see this."

"Do you suppose the commander would mind if we did take a look inside?" Priscilla inquired.

"Won't hurt to try. But let's pretend we're just a couple of curious travelers, just in case good old Archer might have told somebody about me."

Geoffry knocked lightly on the door. It was opened by a young British officer, splendidly uniformed in red coat and white breeches.

"Yes?" he inquired. "The Commandant isn't in right now. Can I be of any assistance?"

"No, I guess not," Geoffry said, then added: "But would you mind if we took a quick peek inside your headquarters? Wasn't this place formerly a private home?"

"Why yes, so it was," the officer replied. "When Colonel Carlton was looking for a place to stay, he was intrigued by the stone floor and fireplace in this building. Said the floor reminded him of one in his own manor house, back in Leeds. And since the place didn't seem to belong to anyone, he decided to make it his headquarters. We've been here ever since."

"It truly is a beautiful floor, with all those different color tones in the design and everything," Priscilla agreed, with a slight wink that only Geoffry could see. "I wonder who could have built it?"

"Obviously a trained stone mason, to turn out something this fine," the officer answered. "Probably died during the 'starving time,' I suspect. Too bad, actually, after all of his skilled work."

"Yes, isn't it though?" Geoffry could barely suppress a grin. "But I'm glad you've been able to make such good use of the place. And thank you for satisfying our curiosity." He shook hands with the genial young officer, then escorted Priscilla back outside and toward the gates of the fort.

"Oh Geoffry, what a *treat* to see your old home!" Priscilla exclaimed as they headed toward the dock. "And what a beautiful floor! I've never seen anything more elegant!"

Geoffry emitted a pleased laugh. With an exaggerated bow, he mimicked, "Why thank you, my dear! I wonder who could have built it?" Both enjoyed a moment of amusement before Geoffry continued, "But if you really did like it,

Priscilla, maybe I can build a floor just like it for our new trading post. Or an even better one, if we can find the right stones."

They strolled back to the trading ship hand in hand, their spirits high. After finding a space at the ship's railing, they watched with interest as the huge stack of hogsheads of tobacco that had been loaded aboard was lashed firmly to the deck, the hold obviously already being full. While they waited together, observing final preparations before resuming their journey, Priscilla snuggled close, her eyes brimming with love. "It's *wonderful* being married to you, Geoffry, and getting to share all of these adventures! I'm so very happy we found each other!"

Her words brought tears of joy to Geoffry's eyes, and he held her in a tight embrace. "There's no way I can *possibly* tell you how much you mean to me, Priscilla! And to think I get to spend the rest of my *life* with you ~ it's almost too much!"

The mood of harmonious affection was broken as the ship's captain barked out sailing orders and all hands jumped to their assigned tasks. Slowly, steadily the trading ship turned down river, setting forth on a voyage bound to bring unknown risks and challenges. But the young couple standing at the rail remained serene, content in the happiness they had found in each other. Together, it appeared, they were confident that they could not only *meet* the challenges before them but could perhaps turn them into *opportunities* as well!

Chapter 27

▼

* * * * *
Five Weeks Later
* * * * *

"Can you believe it, Priscilla? Our last day at sea, after all this time?" Geoffry's smile reflected in the polished square of tin that served as a mirror. The grin surrendered to frustration, however, as he struggled with the knot of his ribbon bow tie.

"Here, Geoffry, let me help you with that." With a few deft twists and tugs, Priscilla straightened the wayward tie. "There! Now you look like a true English squire." Her luminous blue eyes glowed with approval. "You do cut a fine figure in those clothes, you know. Like you've *always* been an aristocrat."

Geoffry greeted her assessment with a self-conscious chuckle. "Why thank you, my dear! Just so I don't look like one of those snobbish dandies we had back there in Jamestown." His strong arms encircled Priscilla in an affectionate embrace. "But no matter what, I'll always be happy to walk in the shadow of the most beautiful woman I've ever known. You truly are something special!"

Pleased yet embarrassed at his high praise, Priscilla deftly steered the conversation in a new direction: "Well, shall we just stand here and compliment each other all day, or had we better get on down to breakfast? Since this is our very last day aboard, we don't want to be late, do we?"

They hurried from their cabin to the officer's dining quarters and settled into their customary seats at the heavy oak table. Early in the voyage, they had been invited to dine with the Captain and ship's officers, an offer they had happily accepted.

During breakfast, talk centered mainly on the anticipated mid-morning docking, though some of the officers were already exchanging ideas about the trading ship's next voyage, as well. But as their morning meal was concluding, the Captain turned to address the young couple: "There's a little something I wanted to mention to you before we land, Mr. and Mrs. Payne, so that you can be prepared. It's something all of us here have come to expect, and frankly, to *enjoy* by now, though I'll have to admit it also makes us a little sad."

He paused momentarily, then continued: "When we tie up at the wharf in London, you'll probably notice a small elderly woman wandering around the docks, waiting to greet us. It never fails! She's been there regularly for a couple of years now. It seems she greets every single incoming trading ship. She stands at the gangplank as people disembark, and she asks every person leaving the ship the same question: "Has ya seen my Billy? Has ya, now?" Over and over, she keeps asking: "Has ya seen my Billy?" And there's always so much *hope* in her eyes, we really hate to disappoint her! So we've all got in the habit of telling her. "No, we haven't seen your Billy, madam, but I'm sure he'd like for you to have this," and then we give her a schilling or two. She looks so grateful when she gets the coins! Maybe they help take away some of her sadness, or maybe they just make it possible for her to keep hanging around the docks to ask her question. Now, I don't have any idea who she is or where she lives or who this Billy is or anything, but she'll be right there, you can count on it!"

Both Geoffry and Priscilla listened to the Captain's words in total amazement, unable to *believe* what they were hearing! But both seemed to grasp its potential significance at once!

"You say she always asks for her *Billy?*" Geoffry turned to Priscilla. "You don't suppose...."

"Oh Geoffry, it *must* be! It's just *got* to be *our* Billy's <u>Mum</u>! Who else could it *be*? Oh Geoffry!"

Trying to contain his growing excitement, Geoffry described briefly for the Captain and his officers how he and Billy Bascomb had come to end up in Virginia, and how he had promised to tell Billy's Mum just what had happened there. When he finished, Priscilla added, "I'm just *sure* that lady *has* to be asking about *our* Billy, Captain! Oh, I'm so happy you told us about her!" Both the Captain and his officers nodded in agreement, seeming pleased at the possibility of a plausible solution to their on-going "mystery".

Needless to say, Geoffry and Priscilla returned to their cabin in a state of jubilant euphoria. They made a quick final check of their belongings to be sure all was in readiness for disembarking. Then, full of eager anticipation, they hurried to the main deck, where they stood at the rail anxiously watching the passing shoreline, impatient to finally reach the London docks. Not only would this mark the end of their journey, but possibly, just *possibly* it might provide the means for Geoffry to fulfill his strongly held and deeply felt obligation to Billy as well.

All of the weeks spent at sea appeared like fleeting moments compared to the time it seemed to take to traverse those final miles up the English Channel and for the ship to make its approach to the hustling docks, where it was secured in preparation for disembarkation. Geoffry's keen gaze continued to sweep the wharf, scanning everywhere in search of the mysterious lady. Priscilla stood close, trying to assist him in their quest.

Then Geoffry gave a sudden shout: "*There*, Priscilla! There she is, *right over there!*" He pointed toward a stack of wooden boxes. "See that tiny little lady standing next to those crates? I'll just *bet* that's Billy's Mum! It *has* to be!"

"Oh, I think you're *right*, Geoffry! But she looks so small, so frail, doesn't she? Do you suppose she really *could* be the same Mum that Billy talked so much about?"

"I'm almost *certain*, Priscilla! That's just *got* to be her! Who *else* would stand there day after day for all this time, like the Captain said, asking about 'her Billy'?"

An idea flashed into Priscilla's thoughts: "If that really *is* Billy's Mum, Geoffry, why don't we share some of our pearls with her? I'm sure we have more than we'll need for our trip. That way, maybe she can finally begin to have the life Billy *wanted* for her, one that's not so hard, even though she won't have her Billy or any of that gold he hoped to find. And we can always find more pearls back home, for our own needs."

"That's a *great* idea, Priscilla! It really is! I'd *like* that! Maybe that way we can help Billy fulfill his *dream* for the Mum who always took such good care of him."

While they talked, Geoffry kept searching his pockets, becoming more and more agitated as he did so. "But I can't seem to *find* our pouch of *pearls*, Priscilla! Where could I have *put* it? Do you remember seeing the little bag this morning? I just can't find those pearls *anywhere!*" Geoffry's voice reflected an edge of panic.

"Are you sure you took the pouch out of our secret hiding place before we left the cabin, Geoffry? I don't see how they could be *lost*. I'm just *sure* they aren't."

Stopping a moment to reflect, Geoffry slapped his palm to his forehead. "Of course! That's it, Priscilla! In our rush to get to the main deck, I forgot all about picking up the pearls! Thank you, thank you, Sweetheart! What would I ever do without you?" He rushed off to retrieve their "treasure," calling out a hasty, "I'll be right back!"

By the time he returned, triumphantly waving the little buckskin pouch, Priscilla and Geoffry were among the last passengers to descend the ship's gangplank. But sure enough, as they reached the dock, the diminutive figure they had seen moved forward to intercept them. In clothes badly worn, with a faded shawl covering her thin shoulders and a bonnet fringed in tatters of faded lace framing her face, she approached resolutely to pose her question: "Has ya seen my Billy? Has ya, now?" The words were plaintive, spoken almost mechanically, yet in her eyes there still shone the dim spark of hope.

"Pardon me, ma'm. Did you say your son's name is *Billy*? Could it possibly be *Billy Bascomb*? And did he always call you his *Mum*?" Geoffry was hesitant, not certain exactly how he would relay the heartbreaking message he so dreaded to deliver.

"Yes, m'lord, yes indeedy! Billy Bascomb! That there's the name o'my lovin' son, it is, Lord bless 'im. An' a right good lad he is, too, no mistake! Went off to find 'im a fortune in Virginny, he did, just so's he could make a better life for his ol' Mum! Yesiree!" She paused, sighing deeply. "But ya knows, I ain't heard nary a *word* from 'im these many years, I ain't!" A look akin to desperation glistened in her dark eyes, fear of the worst challenging the innate optimism. "Does ya happen to know where my Billy's *at,* sire? Has ya possible *seen* 'im? Has ya, now?".

Geoffry took a deep breath, then began: "Yes, Mrs. Bascomb, I *did* know your son Billy! And a better man never lived, believe me! He loved you so *much!* But I'm afraid I have really sad news for you, ma'm. You see, there was a lot of *sickness* over there in the New World. And Billy came down with that dreaded malaria!" He paused. "We've *both* suffered a terrible loss, Mrs. Bascomb. You've lost a wonderful son, and I lost the best mate a man could ever have!"

For a long moment "Mum" Bascomb stood completely still, stunned, as though unable to fathom the *reality* of what Geoffry was telling her, the *finality* that would mark an end to her years of hopeful waiting. Then the frail shoulders slumped, and tears spilled from the tired eyes. As comprehension penetrated, the frail body trembled with quiet, uncontrollable sobs.

Swiftly Priscilla moved forward to hold the fragile frame in a warm, tender embrace, murmuring quietly, "I'm so *sorry*, Mrs. Bascomb, I'm so very sorry we had to bring you this terrible, sad news!"

Geoffry reached out to gently enfold both women, assuring the distraught mother, "*We're* here to help you *now*, Mrs. Bascomb. We're going to make sure you'll be all right. Your Billy died helping to save my life, and I'll never forget that! *Never!* Maybe in some small way I can try to take his place. He was such a very special man!"

Slowly, Mum Bascomb raised her head, eyes bright with gratitude behind the tears. Geoffry put his arm around the slight shoulders as he added, "Please come with us now, Mum Bascomb. Let's go find some place where we can *talk*. I have **so much** I need to tell you!"

-The End-

978-0-595-34898-5
0-595-34898-X